# The Stones

## of

# Burren Bay

Library and Archives Canada Cataloguing in Publication

Title: The stones of Burren Bay / Emily De Angelis.
Names: De Angelis, Emily, author.
Identifiers: Canadiana (print) 20230572391 | Canadiana (ebook) 20230572405 | ISBN 9781988989792
  (softcover) | ISBN 9781988989815 (EPUB)
Subjects: LCGFT: Novels.
Classification: LCC PS8607.E213 S76 2024 | DDC C813/.6—dc23


Printed and bound in Canada on 100% recycled paper.
Cover Artwork: Emily De Angelis
Author Photo: Trish Roberts


Published by:
Latitude 46 Publishing
info@latitude46publishing.com
Latitude46publishing.com


We acknowledge the support of the Ontario Arts Council for their generous financial support.

ONTARIO ARTS COUNCIL
CONSEIL DES ARTS DE L'ONTARIO

an Ontario government agency
un organisme du gouvernement de l'Ontario

# The Stones of Burren Bay

by Emily De Angelis

46

*To My Parents...*

*grounded and centred*
*in debris of place and time*
*stones encircle me*

# Of Wood and Stone

*by Emily De Angelis*


She plants a seedling
in a divot of rich, warm soil,
with hopes and dreams
of a sturdy trunk, long limbs
and copious green leaves to drink the sun.

She circles the hole with
limestone shards—
stones to mark the spot,
some sharp and pointy
others worn smooth by wind and rain.

The stone circle sits.

She waters and feeds her sapling
watches it grow ring on ring,
a toughening of bark
around its core
taproot growing toward gravity.

And still the stone circle sits.

She reclines under her tree
in its summertime shade,
picnics and books
blankets and naps
swinging high from its branches.

And still the stone circle sits.

She cuts down her tree in its old age,
hundreds of linear feet of wood
for fire and furniture
for a small narrow box
to hold a painter's brush.

And still the stone circle sits.

She consumes her tree and its utility,
beams concealed beneath stone and metal,
chairs rotting in the damp of old lighthouses,
dovetailed joints burning to ash
in a blistering burn of flame.

And still the stone circle sits.
For aeons.

# CHAPTER 1

Norie Lynch had never watched someone die before, especially someone she loved like she loved Grandma Johanna. Squirming on the tall, sticky vinyl chair beside her grandmother's bed, she tried to find room for her long and lanky 15-year-old body. Tucked beside her was a sketchbook and a large zip-up pencil case she had made from a worn pair of denim jeans on an old, second-hand sewing machine. She called it her artist's bag of tricks—big enough to carry her graphite pencil collection, four different kinds of erasers and a pencil sharpener. Other tools came and went from the bag as she needed them: paint brushes, small paint palettes, coloured pencils, markers, ink pens and nibs. Today it carried a brand-new tin of charcoal pencils and a small container of compressed charcoal sticks. She intended to use charcoal as the medium for the year-end project in her course at the art gallery this September. The young woman at the art store convinced her to buy a blending stump and a couple of tortillons as well, telling

Norie that she should learn how to use the tools if she really wanted to properly work with charcoal. She dug around in the bag and pulled out a pencil and gum eraser then opened her sketchbook to a clean page. She let her eyes wander around the room for the right thing to sketch.

Norie hated coming to the nursing home. She hated the smell of commercial cleaning products mixed with urine and unwashed bedding that permeated the hallways. She hated the unnaturally bright fluorescent lights and the lack of colour in her grandmother's room. She hated the institutional art hanging in the blank spaces on the walls. Her mother, Alice, came most days, after work and on her days off. She worked constantly, two sometimes three jobs at a time. Sometimes, on Sundays, her father made an appearance, but he was always too busy, or too tired or too whatever to stay for long. Not surprising for a man who couldn't keep a job.

Norie continued to survey the room looking for inspiration. Her mother had made a feeble attempt to make the room seem more homey and less institutional, but she didn't really have the skills for decorating a home let alone a nursing home room. She didn't seem to have many skills for a lot of things, but she did make sure Gram had some of her belongings with her. The bed Grandma Johanna was laying in was her own. It was moved from her old house so at least she would be comfortable lying in the familiarity of the lumps and hollows of her old mattress. Her dresser, nightstands, and cedar chest crowded the tiny space, but made it feel like Gram's place. Norie hated coming to the nursing home, but she loved Gram.

When Grandma Johanna was forced to sell her house and move into the care home months ago, after the first major stroke, Norie and her parents helped her to sort through years and years of treasures tucked into every nook and cranny. In the end she could only keep a few things. She kept the jewellery box Norie's Grandpa

Jack made for her, their wedding picture, a framed photo of Norie as a baby, and a few favourite unicorn statues from her extensive collection. Of course, Norie's father insisted on selling anything he could and stashing the money away in a separate bank account. He had a guy, he said, who dealt in antiques. Rory Lynch always had a guy. Her grandmother maintained that not everything was an antique, but he insisted on trying to sell everything he could. The government might get the money from the sale of her house to pay for the nursing home, he said, but they weren't entitled to the little bit of extra he could get for her antiques and vintage belongings. Norie doubted the existence of the bank account and didn't think anyone else but Rory Lynch ever saw that little bit extra he was talking about. In the end her grandmother and mother gave in. They always did.

Norie's eyes settled on her grandmother lying still and quiet. Her sketchbook was full of drawings of her grandmother's small form swaddled in the old quilt Great-Grandmother O'Carroll had made of mismatched, pale squares of cloth sewn together and mounted on a white cotton backing. In the last month, Grandma Johanna had many mini strokes. The staff called them TIAs, but Norie had no idea what that stood for. What she did know was that her grandmother was not getting better. She came every single day after school to keep her grandmother company. Then school ended for the summer, and Norie kept coming. It's not like she had a life anyway. With no friends, no one she could connect with at school, she had always felt like she existed on the edge of everything. Eventually she decided to just stay there—on the outside looking in. With Gram though, Norie always felt a connection. They shared a love of objects—things old and familiar that felt pleasant and satisfying in their hands. They shared a love of story. Norie could listen for hours to her grandmother talk about her own childhood or tell stories about their ancestors coming to Canada from Ireland. And they shared a love of art. Her grandmother had some artistic ability, but she had given up on drawing and painting after her husband passed away. She said creating beauty was just too difficult when the love of your life was gone. She was a huge champion of Norie's artistic development though and encouraged every attempt Norie made to learn and create.

Norie gripped the pencil in her hand and started sketching her grandmother yet again. Sometimes she sketched her grandmother's face, her translucent skin slack with sleep around her mouth and eyes. Sometimes she sketched her grandmother while she was awake. Norie had come to appreciate those clouded eyes and her wrinkled smile. Gram had moments of clarity, but not many now. When she was awake, she found it difficult to speak, slurring and drooling as her tongue struggled to form sounds and words. Her right side was impaired so she couldn't write either. The doctor said stroke victims who couldn't talk often struggled with written language too. But one afternoon Norie put her sketch pad and pencil on the bed to get a glass of water and when she returned her grandmother had the pencil in her hand sketching out little rough pictures of things around the room. Norie realized they could communicate in simple pictures. She brought a small sketchbook and a few pencils to leave with her grandmother. She called it the talking book as the two of them learned to express themselves in a different way.

Norie focused on Grandma Johanna's hands laying on top of the quilt. She noticed how hands changed over time. Her own were soft and supple—smooth, pink skin held taut over the bones and muscles of her fingers and palms. Her nails painted coal black were smooth and shiny. Her mother's hands were thicker, skin still taut but red from exposure to cold and chemicals, age spots beginning to form and freckle on top. Her nails were ridged and bare. Grandma Johanna's hands were gnarly, knuckles swollen with arthritis and years of wringing mops and dish cloths. Like the skin on her face, it seemed translucent with veins and tendons visible like elastics under plastic wrap. She used to always have her nails done, usually in shades of bright pink or coral and peach. But not since the stroke. Now they were unmanicured, dull and brittle. Deeply intent on drawing hands, Norie didn't notice her grandmother waking up until she started making hoarse, breathy sounds—an attempt at speaking before she realized she couldn't.

"Hey, Gram. Glad you finally decided to wake up and visit with me." She moved to help Grandma Johanna sit up comfortably in her bed, arranging pillows around her small body for support. Her grandmother smiled and nodded and then frowned in apparent confusion. Norie bent over to look directly into her grandmother's eyes. "Are you okay? Do you need something?"

She stared ahead for a few moments, and it seemed to Norie that she was trying to remember something. Maybe something that happened earlier in the day. Maybe something from a dream. Then Grandma Johanna motioned for the talking book sitting on the nightstand. The two of them had been perfecting their rather imperfect communication system for a few weeks now, but this was the first time Norie's grandmother had requested the book so urgently. Norie opened the sketchbook and helped to place the pencil in her grandmother's left hand—the length of the pencil resting in the web space, thumb and forefinger gripping it as tightly as possible. She started to sketch quickly while Norie stood patiently waiting for her to finish. Norie had learned not to interrupt while her grandmother was talking on the page.

Grandma Johanna, with a series of overlapping rectangles joined at their corner, seemed to be sketching a long and narrow container of some kind. It was impossible for Norie to tell the dimensions of the box from a sketch and her grandmother wasn't finished drawing yet. Patience, Norie reminded herself. Her grandmother sketched quick short lines on the long side of the box. Wood grain, maybe, thought Norie. She drew a second, one dimensional rectangle hovering over the box and Norie instantly thought it might be a lid.

"Are you drawing a box? A wooden box maybe?" Grandma Johanna nodded her head up and down as best she could, excited by Norie's recognition of her sketch. She attempted to point repeatedly at Norie's own larger sketch pad laying at the foot of the bed, but damage from the stroke made it difficult for her to raise her arms.

"Well, you said it was a box, so what does it have to do with the sketch book?" Grandma Johanna continued to nod up and down. She started to sketch again and drew what looked like two long strings coming out of the bottom of the box.

"Okay it's a box. A box with ties, maybe?" Again, Grandma Johanna nodded her head up and down. "Is there something you need that's in a box? In this room somewhere?" She started to make noises again and shook her head from side to side. "No. Not something you need from a box." Norie paused for a moment then said, "You want me to get some kind of box that is in the room somewhere." Grandma Johanna smiled and drew a large check mark on the page of the talking book. "Do you remember where it is?" Gram looked confused and uncertain. "Okay," said Norie, "Let's play a game of Hot and Cold."

Beside her grandmother's large check mark in the talking book, Norie drew a large X. "I'm going to move around the room, and you point to the check mark if you think I'm close to what you want and the X if I'm far away. Okay?" Her grandmother gazed down at the sketchbook for a few moments then nodded. Norie started at the door of the room and her grandmother pointed to the X on the page. As Norie got closer to the window and the cedar chest that sat on the floor beneath it, her grandmother was noticeably excited, her pencil shifting to the check mark. She remembered.

"Is it in the cedar chest," she asked, and Grandma Johanna shook her head up and down vigorously. "Okay then, let's see what's in here." Norie lifted the lid of the chest, and the soft close hinges kept the cover upright against the wall while she searched through the contents. The chest was mostly filled with winter clothes that her mother stored over the summer because there wasn't enough room in the closet. There were sweaters and pants, long sleeved tops and a couple of light jackets. Norie took them out and placed them on the foot of the bed while her grandmother watched. On the bottom of the chest were a couple of photo albums. Norie decided to pull those out and store them in the bottom of the nightstand so she and Grandma Johanna could look at them later. All that was left sitting at the bottom of the cedar chest was a wooden box about five or six inches wide and maybe a foot long.

"Yes!" She picked it up and turned toward her grandmother. "This is it, right?" Her grandmother nodded excitedly, a string of drool sliding to and fro from her chin, dripping in a long string onto her floral nightgown. Norie sat the box on the window sill, repacked the clothes and shut the lid. She placed the box on the bed between her and her grandmother. It was rustic, plain and simple in its style, aged to a reddish gold, and warm and smooth to the touch. A fine grain stretched along the wood of the lid and the sides of the box in horizontal wavy lines. Thin, almost brittle, leather straps were tied around it.

"So, what is this, Gram?" Grandma Johanna touched the box gingerly, running her fingertips along the surface, letting the ends of the leather straps cascade through them. She motioned for Norie to remove the top. Norie untied the straps, and a memory of the boot laces Grandpa Jack used to bundle collections of old magazines he wanted to keep flashed through her mind. Norie smiled to herself as she examined the lid. No hinges. No clasp. Grandma Johanna made a horizontal sweeping movement with her hand,

and Norie realized that the lid must slide off. She felt around the top edge of the box and found a small, rounded bump protruding from the surface with a groove carved into it big enough to get a hold of with her fingertips. She pulled and the lid slipped forward along grooved tracks opening the interior of the box. It smelled of old wood and oil. The underside of the lid and the interior of the box were a pale yellow from the lack of sunlight and air. The only item in the box was an old paintbrush. The rounded bundle of bristles was coarse and stiff, and appeared to be affixed to the wooden handle with a band of leather or cloth. Norie looked up at her grandmother who by now was beaming. She nodded and pushed the box toward Norie.

"Is this a painter's toolbox, Gram?" Grandma Johanna nodded yes. She clumsily grabbed for the talking book and drew two stick figures—one large and one small. She pointed to the small one and then pointed at herself. "That's you, right?" Grandma Johanna nodded. Then she pointed at the larger figure. "Is that your mom?" Again, she nodded. Then she drew one more figure a little larger than the mother figure and pointed to it. "Your father?" Gram shook her head. Norie thought for a moment. "Your grandmother?" Grandma Johanna got excited, incoherent grunts coming from her throat trying to form an explanation. Norie understood and she couldn't believe what her grandmother was telling her. "This was your grandmother's artist's box? My Great-Great Grandmother-O'Carroll's?" By now Grandma Johanna was beside herself. She was nodding her head and making unintelligible noises. But her emotions behind the chaos were very clear. She was pleased that Norie had figured out the mystery.

"It's got to be over a hundred years old." Norie recalled Gram's stories of the O'Carroll family's history. "Great-Great Grandmother-O'Carroll must have brought it with her from Ireland when she came. Oh my God! I can't believe it!" She looked at the box and then back to her grandmother. "How come I've never seen it before? Why didn't I see it when we were packing up the house?" Grandma Johanna turned back to the talking book. She drew one small figure and pointed at Norie. Norie smiled and said, "That's me." Her grandmother nodded yes. She drew another figure slightly bigger. "That's mom." Then she drew a very large figure with a zigzag line through its circular head. Norie understood immediately. "You and mom kept it hidden from Dad so he couldn't sell it." It wasn't a question, just a sad statement of fact. The two of them fell silent. After a few moments Grandma Johanna pushed the box in Norie's hands moving it closer to her chest.

"You want me to keep it?" Grandma Johanna nodded yes and then drew a large, squiggly heart on a blank page in the talking book. "Oh Gram, thank you so much." She carefully gathered her grandmother into a warm, gentle hug whispering into her ear, "I'll keep it safe. I promise"

She released her grandmother and glanced down at the box resting in her lap. Norie was now the guardian of a piece of family history, a long history of creativity and beauty secreted in an old wooden artist's box. The box was now a part of her own history. She glanced back to her grandmother, touched by her trust and kindness, but Grandma Johanna's eyes were again unfocused, dull and cloudy as she stared off into some distant time and place Norie couldn't go.

# CHAPTER 2

If Norie thought watching her grandmother die was difficult, experiencing her death was excruciating. She was by herself at the nursing home the moment Grandma Johanna passed. She slipped off silently while Norie was reading an article aloud from her cellphone about the almanac predicting an early winter. The pencil Gram was holding in her fingers, the one she used to draw her words, slipped from her grasp and fell to the floor. Norie heard the sharp sound of the wood hitting the terrazzo tile and the clatter of it rolling under the cedar chest. In a panic, she buzzed the nurses and stood back while they attended to her grandmother but there wasn't anything they could do to bring her back. The early winter the almanac predicted started that moment. And it was only late September.

The following days were a flurry of activity—funeral arrangements, removing Grandma Johanna's belongings from the nursing home, and paperwork. There wouldn't be a service or celebration of life. Grandma Johanna knew there wasn't any money for that. She had left just enough money in trust with her lawyer to pay for cremation and burial in the same plot as Grandpa Jack. Norie watched as her mother moved through all the tasks silently. She hadn't shed a single tear, and she didn't do much to comfort Norie either. Her father's behaviour was worse. She was sure he came to help at the nursing home because he was sniffing around for more stuff to sell. He stalked around the small room, dark eyes darting here and there for salvageable items. He wasn't a large man, his narrow shoulders the same width as his hips, his legs shorter than his torso. His black hair, streaked with a few lines of grey, was too long for his thin face and in desperate need of a cut and style. He added bits of Gram's belongings to two boxes on the bed. Norie had managed to sweep the quilt from the top of the bedding and gather it into her arms before her father sat them down. He tossed in unicorn statues on top of the miscellaneous things he had already pilfered, not even taking care to wrap them in newspaper first to protect them from breaking.

"I think I can sell this stuff on the weekend," he said without so much as a trace of grief in his voice. He looked over at Norie's mother who was silently and carefully looking through her mother's jewellery box. His eyes narrowed, and his thin mouth tightened for a moment. Norie could see her mother had found the cameo that Gram often talked about. It was a gift from Grandpa Jack when they got married. Alice cupped it gently in her hands, rubbing her thumbs against the cool, amber agate it was carved from. "Isn't there some kind of old cameo in there?" Her father moved toward Alice, his face now pleasant, catching a glimpse of it in her hands. He was on the attack. "That's got to be worth a pretty penny."

"I'm keeping the cameo." Her words were abrupt but full of defiance as Alice turned and stared down her husband. Norie stood looking back and forth between her parents. She clutched her grandmother's quilt tightly to her chest like a breastplate of protection, uncertain of what would happen next. Her father was not one to be told no or denied anything, and her mother had perfected the art of giving in. Their eyes locked for a moment before her father spoke.

"Whatever...we'll talk about it later. Is there anything else in there?" He moved into Alice's space, forcing her to step away from the jewellery box. He closed the lid and lifted it onto the bed. "I can go through this later." As he turned around surveying the room, Norie quickly folded the quilt and laid it beside her backpack. She froze when she heard him say, "Wasn't there some old box Johanna had from her grandmother?"

"I don't know if we kept that," her mother answered as Norie held her breath. Alice was lying. Her mother had been the one to unpack everything into the room. She would have known the old box was in the cedar chest.

"I'm sure we did. Your mother would never have let that out of her sight." He started opening drawers in the dresser, searching through her grandmother's undergarments and nightgowns. Norie's stomach heaved and twisted as she watched her father invade Grandma Johanna's most private and intimate belongings.

"Maybe it's in the cedar chest." As Norie spoke she could feel her mother's gaze shift from her father to her. When their eyes met, her mother's expression was a curious mixture of horror and anger. They watched as Rory emptied out the chest and then, finding nothing, shoved it all back in without care—garments unfolded, sleeves and pant legs sticking out from under the lid.

"Nope, nothing in there." Norie's father turned toward the nightstand. "I guess you want these photo albums too?" Her mother was standing still, in shock about the missing box, so Norie stepped forward.

"I want those. Gram and I used to go through those photos all the time." She moved around the bed and took the albums from her father's hands. He continued searching through the nightstand drawers, unceremoniously dumping the contents into the box, on top of all the other things that belonged to Grandma Johanna. The small sketchbook that Norie and her grandmother used to talk to each other fell into the box. Norie reached in and grabbed it. "I want this too." Her father saw no value in the book, so he grunted dismissively and emptied the contents of the second nightstand drawer into a box.

"Well, I told the guys at Bobbie's shop to meet me here to give me a hand moving all this stuff with their truck. They should be here in a few minutes. You two take the car home, and I'll meet you there later."

Norie and her mother left the nursing home for the last time with the few bits and pieces of Grandma Johanna they could save gathered in their hands or stuffed in a purse and backpack. A lifetime reduced to some photos, a quilt, a sketchbook, and a cameo pendant. Her mother said nothing as they moved through the hallways. Nurses and PSWs stopped and gave their condolences. Norie smiled meekly and hugged people the entire way to the front door, but her mother maintained the same stoic demeanour she showed in Gram's room, only nodding politely at the staff as they said their goodbyes. Once in the car Alice turned on Norie.

"Where is it?" Her voice was uncharacteristically assertive, her gaze intense, her shoulders squared. "I know my mother's antique artist's box was in the cedar chest. I put it there. Where is it?" Norie was unsettled by her mother's reaction.

"Gram gave it to me a couple of months ago." Alice's countenance changed immediately, and her shoulders drooped as she collapsed into the seat of the car. She let out a long breath and rubbed her temples with her fingertips.

"She said she wanted me to keep it safe, so that's what I intend to do."

"Just don't let your father know. He'll sell it off in a heartbeat."

"I won't. He'll have to steal it from me now."

"I wouldn't put it past him," said her mother with resignation as she started the car.

Norie wasn't about to give into her father the way her grandmother and mother usually did. But her mother was right. If he found out she had the antique box, he would be relentless in his pursuit of it.

Norie glanced at her mother as she drove out of the nursing home parking lot. Her relationship with Alice was distant at best. There were a million examples. They didn't do the usual mother-daughter things, no shopping for clothes or spa days. Her mother gave her money for those things, sometimes. They never went to mother and daughter occasions. Never went to movies together. On the rare occasion that her mother made it to a school event, she was usually late, showing up in her uniform from work. Not once could Norie remember her mother asking her about school—her studies, her marks or what she wanted to do when she grew up. At best, her mother would scan her report card each term and tell her she was doing a good job. But nothing else. Their relationship was not close, and Norie didn't really understand why. There weren't any big fights. Norie was a good student. A good person. A good daughter. Maybe Alice was just not good mother material.

Norie's relationship with her father wasn't any better. When she was little, he spoiled her with gifts and treats. But as she grew up and became a teenager, he seemed to resent her somehow. He resented the fact that Norie was not one to cave into what he wanted. And lately, he was rarely home, although it wasn't because of work. He had a hard time keeping most jobs. Alone a lot of the time, Norie had come to appreciate the distance between her and her parents. But she'd always had Gram. Now Norie felt all alone.

By the time they got home, Norie was drained. She and her mother shared a can of soup and then each retreated to their bedrooms. There were no words exchanged between them, just the silence of grief. The finality of packing up Gram's room was heavy on her heart, and she couldn't imagine enduring the cold, dark winter without her. Grandma Johanna was the one bright spot in Norie's life—her grandmother and her art. If it weren't for her art classes at school and at the art gallery, Norie didn't think she'd survive the pathetic shitshow that was her life. She took the talking book out of her backpack and flipped through the pages of conversation they had had over the last few months of her grandmother's life. The shaky sketches Grandma Johanna drew with her nondominant left hand were amazing. She was always able to draw with just enough detail to make Norie understand. The little game of 20 questions they played, to really make her communications clear, was just another part of the process. A game they both enjoyed playing. Norie felt a wave of sadness sweep over her. Wrapped in her grandmother's quilt, she lay back on her pillows clutching the talking book to her chest.

Her brief nap was interrupted by angry voices coming from her parents' bedroom. Norie tiptoed to the door and opened it a crack. She could hear her parents' arguing. That wasn't anything unusual. They argued. A lot.

"I said I was keeping the cameo!" Alice's voice was as defiant as it was earlier at the nursing home.

"Do you have any idea how much it's worth?" Her father's voice was equally forceful. "It could pay rent for a few months, Alice. Be reasonable." Reasonable. That's a laugh, thought Norie. When was her father ever reasonable?

"Rory, please...my mom just died." The pleading was always next. First pleading, then begging, then the final crying fit. Norie could hear her mother start to cry. That's when her father would move in with a gentle voice, all lovey dovey. Then she would always give in.

"I know this is a difficult time, Alice. I'll take it to a pawn shop. I know a guy." Norie rolled her eyes. "That way we can get it back when we have some extra money." Their voices went low and quiet, and she couldn't make out what either was saying. Then finally the bedroom door opened, and her father stepped out. He looked smug as he tossed the cameo in the air and caught it in his hand. She had given in.

Well, Norie promised to herself and Grandma Johanna, she wouldn't give in. She moved back into the safety of her bedroom, shutting and locking the door. She closed the blinds and drew the curtains. Norie pulled the art box from its hiding spot in the back of her closet. The old box was cool to the touch, the soft paleness of the wood reminding Norie of her grandmother's skin. She emptied her backpack of odds and ends she didn't need and slipped the art box inside. Everywhere she went, the art box would go—her art box and her sketchbook. Her ability to express herself in pencil and paint were the only things that really mattered now.

# CHAPTER 3

"Y ou can't have it!"

Norie pushed her arm through the straps of her backpack gripping them in her fingers as the car skidded along the slick shoulder. She could feel the corners of the old wooden box through the worn fabric as she wrapped her other arm around the bag. Grandma Johanna had given it to her! She promised to keep it safe. How the hell did he find out about it? She was so careful all winter. She must have slipped up—left her backpack open in the living room or kitchen. But she didn't think so. Maybe her father suspected all along that she had the box. Maybe he searched her room, her backpack, when she wasn't there, when she was in the bathroom. It didn't matter much now. He was intent on getting it even under false pretences, even if it meant risking their lives in this early spring storm.

"You didn't really want to take me to my art class, did you? It was just an excuse to get me and the box in the car. To get it to

Bobbie! He's a bad mechanic Dad, not a dealer on the Antique Roadshow!" Rain turned to sleet and back again, alternating between splatting and pinging on the cracked windshield of the old car.

"Honey," her father's voice was thick with sweetness, "Bobbie thinks that old box must be worth a small fortune, and he knows a guy. You know we need the money. We'll get you another one, something plastic, so it's light and durable." A large half-ton going too fast for the conditions passed them, throwing up an icy spray against the side of the car.

Her mother leaned from the back seat over the console between Norie and her father, still in her donut shop uniform. She wasn't supposed to be with them. At the last minute, as they were backing out of the driveway, she dashed out of the house and got into the back seat.

"He wants to sell Grandma Johanna's art box," Norie said. "Do something!" she implored, catching her mother's eyes for only an instant before her father turned hard onto the street and gunned it forward.

"Watch the road, Rory! Please!" Her mother pressed. "They just announced on the radio that the conditions are worsening. Maybe we should just go home."

"No, we're already out here. We're going. Bobbie said this guy is only in town today."

"You can go wherever you want, but you aren't selling my box. Grandma Johanna gave it to me." Norie pounded her finger into her chest repeatedly. She owned the box. "We don't need the money. You want it. That's all you think about all the time. Money, money, money. And control. Just like when you took Mom's cameo. Grandma Johanna meant her to have it, right Mom?" Her mother sat mutely, her eyes darting between Norie and her father and back to the road ahead. "Mom! Say something! Tell him he can't do this!" Norie pleaded, but her mother remained silent.

"Listen Norie, sweetheart..." Her father's endearment made Norie sick to her stomach. "I made a promise to Bobbie, and now I have to keep it." He reached to grab the backpack from her lap. The car fishtailed again, but the bald tires found purchase and the car straightened on the road.

"Watch the road!" Her mom pleaded. "Forget about the damn box and pay attention to what you're doing!"

"Alice! Enough!" At his angry command, Norie's mother slid back into her place. "Honora—" She cringed at her father's use of her full name. "You don't have a choice in the matter! I make the decisions in this family."

"Pretty bad ones, if you ask me," Norie retaliated. "If we need the money so badly maybe you should have made a better decision and not quit your job at the mall. Or at the garage. Or at the taxi company. Or—"

"I've had enough out of you too, young lady!" He grabbed for the backpack in her arms, and they struggled over it. The tires hit black ice under the liquid layer of freezing rain and sleet. Norie's father slammed on the breaks, but the rear wheels locked and turned sharply. The car's back end began to rotate, and the car spun forward. It seemed to Norie that time slowed down as they twisted recklessly along the road they shouldn't have even been on. Her body felt the force of the spin, and her eyes tried to keep up with their trajectory. Partially melted snowbanks, trees, hedges, light standards. They spun into and out of her view rapidly, but she saw each object with clarity. Her thoughts about how that could be—how she could see things clearly while they spun violently out of control—were interrupted by the sudden appearance of a pair of headlights immediately in front of them. Her mother screamed. The impact threw Norie forward in her seat, slamming her head against the dash. She blacked out.

The darkness was impenetrable. She struggled to open her eyes before it swallowed her alive, but her eyelids ached with the strain of waking. Her head throbbed. When she relaxed, she found some relief and it seemed to her that giving in to the darkness wouldn't be so bad. Her mother whimpered from somewhere in the blackness beyond the headrest. She was vaguely aware of wind and ice lashing out at the glass and metal entrapping them, of the sizzle of steam from a crushed radiator, of a siren wailing in the distance. There was a crackling, snapping sound and she could feel gentle warming of her toes, a comfortable heat that travelled upwards to her face. Then the warmth smelled wrong—like electric heaters turned on after months of disuse, only worse. The heat intensified rapidly, covering her nose and mouth like a glove and she began to struggle again.

Fire! The car was on fire! She turned her face away, opening her eyes wide searching for an escape. Instead, she found her father's lifeless body slumped over the steering wheel. Blood was running freely from his ear and from a gash on his head. His eyes were open but vacant. She tried to scream but was choked by the increasing smoke and the heat of the flames.

Again, her mother whimpered and groaned. Norie's left arm was awkwardly bent and tangled in the backpack straps. With her right hand she pushed the backpack off her lap to the floor and reached across her body to release the seat belt. Every nerve in her screamed out simultaneously. Pushing through the pain, she undid her seatbelt. She groped for the door handle. She fell from the car as the door swung open. For a moment, she lay curled up on the cold, wet ground, wanting nothing more than to fall asleep. The heat from the growing fire warmed her as she relaxed against the hard pavement. The ice and water on the ground smelled of salt brine and gasoline. Then she remembered her mother.

"Mom…I'm coming Mom." Her whimper was inaudible

through the weather and the wreckage.

Norie pushed herself upright and struggled to stand, swallowing a wave of nausea. She grasped the rear door handle and pulled, stumbling back as the door gave way. She got her footing again and peered into the car. Her mother was splayed across the backseat, motionless, her head close to Norie. In the light of the flames Norie thought she saw her mother's eyes open and then close. She reached into the car, grabbed the hood of her jacket, and pulled. She couldn't budge her. Then she remembered the seatbelt. She reached in past her mother's head to the centre seatbelt buckle and released it. She grabbed the hood again and pulled. Her mother's body slid toward the opening along the vinyl seat. Then, reaching in, she grabbed her mother under her arms, pulling with a strength she shouldn't have even been able to muster. In that moment of giddy hope, the gasoline ignited, and the car was engulfed in flames.

# CHAPTER 4

It's been a year of loss, thought Norie—her beloved grandmother, her deadbeat father, and an antique wooden box that had travelled all the way from Ireland with her Great-Great-Grandmother. And it was all her fault. Norie and her mother stood beside a grave now shared by her grandparents and her father. Alice had been forced to have Rory's ashes buried in the same plot as Grandma Johanna and Grandpa Jack because there wasn't any money to buy a new one. The government death benefit barely covered the cremation. It made Norie sick to her stomach to think that her beloved grandparents were stuck with her father for an eternity. She zipped up the collar of her coat trying to keep the dampness of the day at bay. It looked like rain as grey clouds gathered and obscured the pale blue, early spring sky.

"Perhaps we should be going?" Mrs. Campbell, their neighbour, had driven them to the cemetery the afternoon of the interment. Norie could see how awkward it was for her to be there, but she was kind and willing. Only a handful of people came and went, and most of them were Alice's co-workers. Her father had no living relatives that she knew of. Not a single friend of her father's showed up either. Maybe in the end they weren't really friends. They were just guys her father knew.

"Mom?" Norie's mother stood staring down at the newly mounded pile of earth sitting on top of the grave. "Mom, we have to go." Alice lifted her eyes and gazed at Norie for a moment. They were sunken and bloodshot from weeks of poor sleep. Norie would never have described her mother as beautiful, but her normally clear and smooth skin was now pallid and mottled. Alice nodded and turned to follow Mrs. Campbell back to her car. As they reached the car parked along the cemetery road, a brown, rusted pick-up truck pulled up behind and a small, balding man got out. He was dressed in a worn plaid shirt and beige cargo pants stained with greasy patches of oil. His work boots scraped along the surface of the road as he shuffled toward them.

"Mrs. Lynch?" His voice was small and high pitched. Alice smiled weakly and nodded. "I'm Bobbie Moore. I'm—I was—a friend of your husband." As he held out his hand toward her mother, Norie could see dirt under his nails. His smooth, hairless hand shook.

"Oh yes," said Alice, taking his hand limply. "My husband spoke of you." Norie managed to control her face, keeping the smirk from her mouth.

"Yah, well he and I worked together a lot." Worked. That's rich thought Norie. "I'm sorry I'm late. I just wanted to come and pay my respects."

"Well, thank you Mr. Moore. It was kind of you." Norie could see her mother just wanted to leave.

"You know, all us guys down at the shop really liked Rory. He was a good guy. Do anything for you, you know." Bobbie nodded up and down while he spoke. Who was he trying to convince, she thought. She turned away, unable to accept Bobbie's praise of her father. Both she and her mother stood silently until Mrs. Campbell finally spoke up.

"Mr. Moore, you are just in time to pay your last respects to Mr. Lynch at the grave side. Mrs. Lynch and her daughter are truly exhausted from the day, as you can imagine." Norie smiled at Mrs. Campbell, thankful for her intervention.

"Oh, yah, of course. I'll do that." He moved away from the car and Norie opened the door for her mother to get in. As a last thought, Bobbie turned and added, "If you need anything, anything at all, just let us know. The boys and I are there for you, you know. Rory was a good guy." He then turned and walked off toward the only open grave in the cemetery.

Norie wanted to shout after him that her father was not so good a guy to her and her mother. She wanted to scream across the graves and tombstones that her father had become a leach and a liar. Her father's death and the loss of the art box was on her. She knew that. She was desperate to get to her art class the night of the accident because art felt like the only real, sane thing in her life. She thought she could keep the box a secret. She thought she could outwit her father. That's where she went wrong. That's why she was responsible. It was hubris, like they talked about in English class. Just like Icarus, Norie had flown too close to the sun—too close to Rory Lynch. He had left nothing for his family but a legacy of lies and betrayal. She said none of this. Instead, she crawled into the backseat beside her mother and Mrs. Campbell pulled away from the curb. Shrugging down into her jacket she turned to stare out the window feeling empty and cold as they drove back home.

In the month following her father's death, Norie learned just how irresponsible he had been. Rory Lynch had left a legacy of debt. Lots and lots of debt. Alice had been unable to work since the accident. The kindness of neighbours and the GoFundMe page co-workers set up for them brought in enough food and cash to help Norie and her mother survive for a few months until Alice could return to work. If Alice could return to work. In the early days after the accident Norie wasn't sure about how much her mother made and if it would be enough for them to survive on. She wasn't sure how much rent was. Wasn't sure how much money it would take to pay for the landline and internet bills, electricity, gas, and food. She wasn't sure how much it would cost to replace her cell phone that had been destroyed in the fire. When bills started piling up on the kitchen counter, her parents obviously didn't believe in internet banking, Norie made it her business to find out and put it all on a spreadsheet on her laptop. Seeing the numbers only stressed her beyond belief! How would they survive? How could they survive? Maybe she could get a part time job. Surely her father's pathetic attempts at making money didn't bring in as much as Norie could if she worked a few fast-food restaurant-shifts a week. She would be 16 at the end of the summer. She was ready for a part time job. She wasn't so sure she was ready to support herself and her mother on her own.

Norie moved around the kitchen, a kitchen she now thought of as hers, making dinner for her and her mother. Nothing gourmet, just canned cream of tomato soup and grilled cheese sandwiches. She liked cooking but wasn't ready to cook outside her comfort zone. Besides, she still had some pain and discomfort from her injuries and standing for long periods of time hurt. She was forced to sit down every so often. She had suffered a mild concussion, a strained shoulder and elbow on her left arm, and a huge gash on one of her knees. Once released from the hospital, Alice's physical injuries, mostly burns and abrasions, required care during the day by a homecare nurse. Although the rescue team thought they were lucky to have survived such a brutal accident, Norie was not certain that either of them really survived at all. Her mother was on heavy duty painkillers and drugs for depression. She was snowed—the homecare nurse's term, not hers—most of the time. Administering the drugs at night and in the morning became Norie's job, and the nurse left instructions to follow after Norie lied and said her grandmother would be visiting them daily. During the day she took over running the house. She impersonated her mother on calls to the school to arrange the end of her school year. The Guidance Department decided to give Norie her year based on the work already completed. She was a good student and her marks going into the last months were excellent. She was exempted from final exams and allowed to remain at home for the rest of the year recuperating along with her mother and her fictitious grandmother. She spent her days cleaning, cooking, doing laundry, anything that would keep her busy. Anything but art. Her mother stayed in bed most of the time, occasionally sitting in a chair in the living room in front of the television. Just staring. Always staring.

Norie flipped the grilled cheese sandwiches for the final time. The cheese was oozing and the bread was cooked to a golden brown. She turned off the element and ladled the tomato soup into two mismatched bowls. Nothing matched in this kitchen. The plates, mugs, cutlery, pots, and pans all came from stuff her father scrounged. They must have started their married life with matching dishes, but she had no memory of that. Norie pushed the sympathy cards that had come in the mail to the middle of the table and set spots for herself and her mother. From the door of the kitchen she called her mother to dinner. She slid the cooked sandwiches onto plates and carried them and the bowls of hot soup over to the table and sat down to wait for her mother. Grandma Johanna always insisted they sit down together to eat a meal. Nothing, she said, will get too dry or too cold simply by waiting a few minutes for your loved ones to gather and take a seat. Ten minutes later when Alice hadn't shown up yet, Norie got up and went to her mother's room. She knocked on the door but there was no answer at first. She knocked again.

"Mom?" Norie called through the door. "Dinner's ready."

"I'm not hungry." Her mother's voice was raspy and rough, her vocal cords dry from medication and not talking for hours on end, sometimes days.

"Are you sure? I made tomato soup and grilled cheese."

"I don't want to eat."

Norie stood at the door, a familiar anger rising in her chest. Really. This is the game we're going to play now? She marched back to the kitchen, emptied her mother's soup bowl into the sink and tossed the grilled cheese into the garbage can. Fine, thought Norie, then starve! She moved back to the table and sat down heavily at her spot and started eating. The first few mouthfuls were hardly chewed. Slowly the anger was replaced with anguish, and Norie could barely eat herself. Cleaning up the kitchen would be a welcome distraction, but her body needed to relax first. She needed to sit a moment and let the emotion gripping her muscles and nerves subside before she could move around easily without pain. Aches and pains. Such a weird thing for a 15-year-old to have to consider, she thought. She glanced at the sympathy cards in the middle of the table. There were three which surprised Norie. She had no aunts, no uncles, or cousins. No grandparents. No Grandma Johanna. Who would be sending sympathy cards to them?

The first one was from Norie's teacher at the art gallery. Inside was the typical expression of sympathy and a promise to stop by soon to see how everyone was doing. In the corner of the card was a little hand drawn, stylized picture of a paint brush. It reminded Norie of the pictures her grandmother talked to her with. Quickly she closed the card and stuffed it back in the envelope. The second card was from Norie's school, signed by the principal, vice principal and office staff. The third envelope, the smallest, was pale blue and looked handmade. In beautiful calligraphy across the front was both her and her mother's names and address. Written across the back, in the same elegant script, was a return address for Burren Bay, Ontario. Norie had never heard of Burren Bay before. She carefully opened the envelope and pulled out a card drawn on beautiful blue, matte-finish cardstock. On the front was a knot drawn in black ink, the lines looping around and through each other forming three interlocking shapes. Below the knot was a saying, first written in another language Norie didn't know and then translated into English:

*Ar scáth a chéile a mhaireann na daoine*
In the shelter of each other people survive.

The card, originally blank inside, held a personal message to Alice. The writer expressed sympathy at Rory's passing and hoped that Alice and Norie were doing okay. It went on about how the loss of someone close was always painful, but that the tears shed, and the grief felt are just signs of the deep love people have for each other. The author of the letter indicated that they must try to connect soon and that it had been too long since they had last visited. It was signed, *Dahlia*. In a subscript below her note, Dahlia wrote that if they needed anything, anything at all, to not hesitate to call. She added her phone number at the very bottom of the card.

Norie vaguely remembered meeting Dahlia and her daughter at a coffee shop when she was in elementary school. Dahlia was her mother's one and only friend, at least the only friend Norie knew about. She thought she remembered that the two had gone to university together. As far as she knew it had been years since Alice and Dahlia had last been in contact. Norie had no idea how Dahlia would even know about her father's death. She opened the card again, noticing a scent escaping from inside the folded paper. The card smelled of something sweet and woodsy. It reminded Norie of the perfume Gram liked to wear. The name of if flitted on the edge of her memory.

"Sandalwood!" Norie said out loud. The blue card smelled like sandalwood. It smelled like Grandma Johanna. She opened and closed the card over and over, breathing in the scent of her grandmother and feeling instantly calm. Gram had that effect on people. Norie put the small blue card back into its envelope and carried it to her bedroom. She tucked it into the talking book on her nightstand and returned to the kitchen to clean up.

In the middle of the night Norie was startled awake by a loud crash. She wasn't sure if it was a sound from her nightmares—the sounds of metal bending and twisting and glass shattering—or a sound from somewhere in the house. She leaned over and turned on her lamp. The clock on the nightstand read 2:30am. She sat up in bed and listened. She thought she heard movement and then something fell over. She was up in an instant running to her mother's room. Without knocking, Norie opened the door and turned on the bedroom light. In the corner of her mother's room, behind a rocking chair and an overturned plant stand, she found her mother sitting cross legged against the wall.

"Mom? Are you okay?" Norie approached Alice slowly, cautiously, unsure of what was happening. When her mother didn't answer she moved into the corner and touched her on the shoulder. "How about we get you back into bed?" Her mother looked up at her but didn't answer. Instead, she let Norie help her to stand. Once steady on her feet Norie took her hand and led her back to bed. Alice crawled under the blankets and her daughter tucked them around her. Norie felt like she was caring for Gram all over again. She stood over her mother for quite some time until she heard the soft even sound of her breathing. Thank God, Norie thought to herself. She moved to the end of the bed and righted the plant stand that had fallen over. The pot hadn't held a living plant for some time, so there was only a small mound of dirt on the floor. Norie got the broom and quietly swept up the dry soil and put it in the garbage. Her mother was still sleeping soundly when she exited the room, leaving the door open so she could hear if she got up again.

By the time Norie returned to her own room it was well after three in the morning. She sat on the edge of the bed, her door left open as well, and wondered what she would do next. She wrapped herself in her grandmother's quilt, staving off the chill of night. They couldn't go on like this. Her mother needed to sleep and eat and be normal. This was not normal. It wasn't normal for a 15-year-old to be taking care of a parent like this. Norie glanced at the talking book where she had tucked Dahlia's hand-made sympathy card. At that moment Norie decided she would call. She didn't know what kind of help Dahlia could truly offer living in Burren Bay, wherever that was. But there wasn't anyone else Norie could think to contact for help. All she had right now was a shadow of the one parent she had left. She had absolutely nothing to lose.

# CHAPTER 5

Norie startled awake as the bathroom door banged against her knee. The kid who had been throwing a tantrum in the bus station raced down the centre aisle back to his inattentive mother. Norie rubbed her knee, acutely aware of the newly healed scar under her black, ripped jeans. Her gaze wandered to the scene flashing past the bus window. The early June sun shone on morning dew, animating the leaves and grass as they fluttered in the breeze. She glanced at her mother sitting beside her, unnaturally upright, staring into the space between herself and the next seat.

It had been a challenge to get Alice onto the bus at the station. The noise of the diesel engine and the smell of the exhaust that hung in the air under the covered departure zone had thrown her into a panic. Truth be told, Norie had to do a lot of self-talk to keep her own fear under control. They had been in cars since the accident, but the bus was enormous, smelly and loud. In the time it took to convince her mom to get on the bus, it had filled up leaving only the very back seat beside the bathroom and over the engine vacant. Almost an hour into the ride and her mother was still unsettled.

"Mom, are you okay? Mom? Mom?" Norie touched her hand. The gauze was moist from the burn cream Norie applied liberally that morning. The homecare nurse had shown her what to do in case they couldn't get a nurse to visit Alice in Burren Bay. Her mother's wounds, though healing, were still deep and raw. Alice stirred, blinking her eyes, licking her dry lips.

"Yes," she took a few tentative, deep breaths. "Yes, I'm fine." She turned away to look out the window, adding as an afterthought, "Are you okay?" But she never turned back to Norie for the answer.

"Better than you are," Norie replied with quiet sarcasm, barely hiding her bitterness. Barely hiding her fear. Her mother didn't seem to notice. Norie stared intently at her bitten nails, the black polish chipped along the tips, holding back the tears she had yet to cry. It was going to be a long bus ride.

The bus travelled westward along the Trans-Canada Highway before turning south onto a small single lane highway that wound its way through towns and villages, swathes of dense forest, and rock cuts through the La Cloche Mountain range. Norie learned that Burren Bay was a tiny community on the shore of Manitoulin Island bordered on one side by the Rocky Plain First Nation. She had a vague memory of a day trip to the Island with her grandparents years ago, but she was so little she had no clear impressions of the visit now. Everything she saw online seemed to focus on tourism—art galleries, campsites, concert events and powwows. When she made the early morning call to Dahlia and told her that her mother wasn't doing well and that she was all alone, Norie really had no idea what to expect. Dahlia instantly invited them to come stay with her at the tearoom and lighthouse museum she managed in Burren Bay. She bought their bus tickets online and somehow convinced Alice that this trip would be exactly what she needed. What they both needed. Norie really didn't feel like they had a choice.

Her backpack sat at her feet. A new backpack smelling of freshly manufactured petroleum-based fabric, both fire and water retardant. A backpack without her latest sketch books and her artist's bag of tricks. One without the beginnings of an artist's morgue and notes from Visual Arts for Young Adults, stuffed in a three-inch, navy-blue binder. A backpack without Grandma Johanna's wooden artist's toolbox. She lifted the backpack onto her lap and pulled out the brand-new sketchbook her well-meaning art teacher had given her when she visited a few days before they left for Burren Bay. She opened it to the first blank page as she had done over and over. The white, light weight paper seemed to mock her, taunting her to pick up a pencil and sketch if she dared. But she couldn't. Not now. Maybe not anymore. As the bus wound its way along the narrow highway, Norie stared at the emptiness of the page.

It's your fault. It's your fault. IT'S. YOUR. FAULT.

Finally, she closed the sketchbook and laid her head back against the padded rear wall of the bus.

Almost two hours into the trip the bus came to a stop along a portion of the highway bordered by a fast-moving channel of water. Over the intercom, the bus driver explained that they would be stopped for a few minutes while they waited for the swing bridge to close so that they could cross the North Channel onto Manitoulin Island. A sign posted at the side of the highway indicated that the bridge opened on the hour from Victoria Day weekend until Thanksgiving weekend. Norie watched as two boats with tall masts sailed through the unobstructed opening created by the turned bridge. Although it had been a warm May, the June waters of the channel looked frigid. Foot high swells formed as the wind tore over the surface, leaving blackened crevices where the water swirled, lifted, and fell. When the two boats cleared the bridge, it swung back into place connecting the Island to the mainland. As they crossed the bridge over the cold, roiling water, the metal panels that formed the floor of the structure clattered and banged with the weight of vehicles and movement of tires. Norie couldn't help feeling an affinity for the Island—they were the same. They both stood alone surrounded by rough waters only tethered to solid ground by an old, rickety bridge. She only hoped that if she needed to, she could swim.

They drove into the small town of Little Current. At the Manitoulin Tourist Information Centre, the bus pulled in to allow a few passengers to disembark. The passengers remaining on the bus had the opportunity to use the washrooms in the information centre. Norie was afraid that if she or her mother got off the bus, she wouldn't be able to talk either of them into getting back on. If she got desperate, she could always use the bus washroom. She wasn't that desperate yet. Within fifteen minutes they were back on the road. As the afternoon passed, they travelled narrow highways along farmland, over escarpment and through small towns westward. At times the land was barren with exposed limestone visible on the surface. At other times endless stands of cedar and poplar trees crowded the forest right up to the edge of the highway.

It was late afternoon when the bus arrived in Burren Bay. The sudden whoosh of air brakes startled Norie and her mother from uneasy sleep and they both gasped audibly and clutched the seats in front of them. Norie, embarrassed by her over reaction, quickly lowered her hands and started to gather her belongings. It took her mother a few extra minutes to settle, her hands slowly loosening on the seat in front of her, her breath returning to normal. Even though she had nodded on and off through most of the trip, Norie was exhausted. The bus had lost its air conditioning miles back and the ripped knees in her jeans did little to cool her. Her feet were sweating in the heavy laced boots she wore, and she would have sworn the black eyeliner she put on that morning had melted and run down her cheeks. By now she desperately had to use a washroom.

The diminutiveness of Burren Bay, a hamlet really, struck her instantly as she looked out the window to the bus stop in front of the convenience store, one of the only public buildings, besides the community centre and church. Off in the distance she could just make out the top of an old lighthouse. It was three o'clock and there was barely a soul on the street, except for Dahlia and her daughter Wilhelmina. They looked vaguely familiar to Norie but because they were the only people there, she assumed it had to be them. A man stood alongside them and Norie's throat tightened. She was not expecting anyone other than Dahlia and Wilhelmina.

"Mom, we're here."

"Okay," Alice replied. "Let's go then." The exchange was brief and hollow. Norie stood and let her mother slide to the edge of the bench seat, stand and steady herself to walk the aisle. The empty sketchbook that had been on the seat between them, was pushed along the vinyl surface and over the edge, lodging itself between the seat and the bathroom wall. Norie left it where it fell, gathered their carry-on bags, and turned to follow her mother. They disembarked and instantly Dahlia and Alice embraced. Norie stood in awkward silence. The man who had been standing beside them moved closer, laying his hands on Wilhelmina's shoulders.

Dahlia was a large woman, not fat but tall and wide hipped, with a straight back and squared shoulders. She was dressed in faded jeans two sizes too big, a baggy sweatshirt and rubber boots pulled over her pant bottoms. Her long black hair, streaked with grey, was pulled back off her face exposing a ruddy complexion, skin weathered by sun and wind. Next to this healthy, outdoors woman, her mother was even more pale and skinny.

"Norie." Dahlia moved to embrace her. Quietly, so that only Norie could hear she whispered, "I am so glad you called. Everything will be okay now. I promise." Dahlia loosened her grasp and Norie quickly moved away nodding a quick thank you. Wilhelmina, who had been standing beside her mother with the unidentified man, smiled and nodded. She was taller than Norie and dressed more like her mother than your average 15-year-old. Not a bit of make-up and her hair was curly and unruly.

"You're just in time for tea and a little something," she said, welcoming them. Alice froze as she stared at Wilhelmina and the stranger. Dahlia noticed and turned to face Norie and her mother.

"This is Gibson." She gestured back to where the man stood, and he moved forward tentatively. "He is my husband. My new husband." Gibson nodded and smiled. Alice nodded back. They didn't know Dahlia had remarried. They didn't know he would be here. A husband and a stepfather. Dahlia slid her arm through Alice's. "I baked fresh scones this morning and the kettle has already been boiled. Let's go talk."

They moved along the road up the hill toward the lighthouse, Wilhelmina in the lead. Gibson collected the suitcases from the side of the road where the driver had placed them and followed Wilhelmina. Norie, weighted down with their miscellaneous baggage, followed. As they made their way along the gravel road, she thought she heard someone call her name—a voice moving down through the trees along the shoreline. She stopped and looked around. She had never been here before and the only people who knew her, who would be calling her name, were the four people walking ahead of her on the road. It made no sense that someone was calling her. Months of fatigue were playing with her senses, she thought. Seeing nothing and no one, she decided it was only the wind blowing through the cedar trees, pushing waves onto the shore beyond.

# CHAPTER 6

Nestled in a small, forested area, at the edge of town beyond a tidy, red metal roofed cottage and an old garage, was a small house with a wrap-around porch. It was sided with grey cedar shingles and the white paint on the trim and around the eaves and windows was peeling. On the wide, wooden front door, that didn't seem to match the size of the building, was a sign that read *The Jolly Pot Tearoom and Gift Shop*. The front yard, surrounded by a low, wooden picket fence, was unkempt and weedy. The grass, what there was of it, poked out of the dirt, and the flower beds were filled with dead plants and greenery struggling to grow up through the debris.

The disarray Norie witnessed in the yard continued into the house. Tables and chairs were all stacked on one side of the main room and two or three area rugs were rolled up and placed along one wall of a second inner room. Boxes were scattered here and there in various states of being unpacked. A set of French doors that closed off one room from the other were held back by folk-painted milk cans.

"You'll have to excuse the mess. We've only just started setting up for tearoom season." Dahlia marched Alice ahead to what Norie guessed was the kitchen. Wilhelmina and Gibson moved boxes cluttering the path they were taking.

"I need to go to the washroom," said Norie, lowering the bags she was carrying to the floor just inside the front door.

"It's down this hall, the door at the end." Dahlia gestured toward the hallway without stopping. Norie watched her mother sit down at a long table along a row of windows before making her way through the boxes stacked in the hall. The tiny washroom was also in a state of disorder, with plastic bins shoved into corners and cleaning supplies and rags strewn about.

When she entered the kitchen a few minutes later, it struck her how remarkably different this room was. Here everything was orderly and clean. Open shelves above a sideboard held various labelled jars of loose-leaf teas. Some were as black as licorice, leaves curled tightly into tiny buds. Some looked like bits of dappled leaves and twigs gathered and crumbled into jars. Others reminded Norie of sage coloured moss and lichen dried by the summer sun. The whole room was warmed with the scent of brown sugar, butter, and spices.

"I just got most of this season's new teas that I ordered online." Dahlia busied herself at the counter as she spoke. Gibson, who had been standing silently leaning against the doorframe moved out of the doorway to the other side of the kitchen. He was a big man, tall and muscular, and seemed to fill the kitchen as he leaned against the cupboards. Dahlia continued, "I'm still waiting for some special brews I discovered over the winter. I have a few ideas for this year's blends."

After setting a kettle over the flame of the gas stove, she chose a jar of dark loose leaf, scooping out a measured amount into a white teapot. Norie sat in the kitchen chair closest to the door. She glanced into another room off the hall in the same state of messiness. It looked like an office, but the corner of a bed draped in a dark blue comforter jutted out from behind the door indicating that the small house had many functions. There was an odd collection of photos and prints lining the walls, none of which seemed to be connected by theme or colour or style. A wooden sign with the words *Jolly Pot Teapot Museum* painted on it, hung over a doorknob. A floral print border trimmed both main rooms and continued down the hall towards the washroom. The whistle of the kettle drew her attention back to the kitchen and the two women—one talking nonstop and the other sitting still and quiet. Wilhelmina sat on the opposite side of the table, watching Norie. When their eyes met, Wilhelmina looked down, busying herself with the fringe of one of the placemats that adorned the table. Dahlia poured the freshly boiled water over the tea leaves, put the lid on the pot and turned over a small hourglass timer on the shelf above the stove.

"Three minutes steeping makes the perfect cup of black tea," Wilhelmina stated. Dahlia looked at her and smiled warmly. When her gaze settled on Norie she declared, "My goodness you are the spitting image of your grandmother."

"You knew my grandmother?" Norie looked at her mother.

"Oh sweetheart, your mother and I go back a long way." Her mother flinched and turned to look out the window.

"You have a beautiful place here Dahlia," Alice said, changing the topic. "I guess this month is all about cleaning and setting up for the tourist season?" Norie looked away, irked by Alice's evasiveness, and annoyed by her willingness to talk here and now, while she hardly had two words for Norie over the last few weeks.

"There's a lot to do as I'm sure you could see in the front rooms. We basically wipe away our cozy home and reconfigure it for the tearoom. And there's cleaning and decorating..." Dahlia's voice drifted off as she arranged cups and saucers on a tray and took scones out of a baking tin, placing them on a small platter.

"And all as a newlywed," Alice said and Norie couldn't tell if she was being congratulatory or sarcastic. Gibson nervously shifted his gaze out the window. What was he hiding, Norie thought. She didn't trust him.

"Will I have my own bedroom while I'm here?" Norie's voice interrupted Dahlia's tea preparations and her mother's attempt at subject-changing chitchat.

"You and Wilhelmina are sharing a bedroom. We've been cleaning out the attic room. It's not done yet, but it's livable. It's a calm, peaceful place though. Alice, you will be in the room at the end of the hall."

"That was my old room, but I don't mind sharing." Wilhelmina smiled at Alice and then looked at Norie. "The attic isn't a huge space, but we added a couple of cots and a little dresser we can share." Again, Wilhelmina and her mother shared a smile. Dahlia placed the tea tray on the table and turned to Norie.

"If you want to bring up your stuff, it's just down the hall towards the washroom—last door on the left." Dahlia turned toward Gibson. "Can you show her?" Gibson nodded and smiled at Norie as he moved forward out of the kitchen. "Mind the stairs, they're steep," Dahlia called after them.

Norie jumped at the chance to leave the room but didn't want or need an escort. She hurried out to the foyer, grabbed her travel bag and backpack and wove her way back through the mess in the hall to the attic door. Gibson stood back and let her climb the stairs ahead of him. The attic room ran pretty much the whole length of the house, but at least half of it was full of boxes, suitcases and two old steamer trunks.

"It's not fancy, but it's functional," Gibson said. Norie felt a headache coming on. The room was hot and airless. She moved across the attic to the only window, a tiny porthole at the front of the house looking onto the bay. She struggled to open it.

"Let me," Gibson moved into her space to help, and she stepped out of the way, irritated by his attempt to take over. "The latch sticks." He fiddled with it for a few tense moments until it let go and he pulled the framed glass inward. The slightest of breezes blew in through the screened opening. Norie moved away saying nothing.

"Well, I'll let you unpack and relax a little. I'm sure you're tired from the long bus ride." Then he added, "I'll be taking out the rest of these boxes when I have some time, so you girls will have more space." She said nothing. She listened to his footsteps on the stairs as he quietly left.

Norie stood beside the cot she claimed as her own. She didn't expect Gibson to be there. She thought it would be just her, her mother, Dahlia, and Wilhelmina. She didn't want another husband or father in her life right now. Even if he wasn't her own.

"I'm sorry about what happened to your family." Norie startled at the disembodied voice coming from the stairway. Wilhelmina moved into the dim light. "My mom said you were in a car accident. That your dad died?" Norie could only nod.

"I don't have a father either. He left when I was little." Norie felt a twinge of sympathy.

"Sorry."

"It's okay. At least we have Gibson now. You'll be okay too, you know, eventually." Wilhelmina wandered around the open space between the cots and in front of the little window.

"This is a sacred space, you know. The spirits feel welcome here."

"You mean there are ghosts here?" Norie scanned the room. "It's haunted?"

"No," Wilhelmina giggled, "It's not haunted, just...blessed. Mom says spirits, their energies, are somehow tied to a place or a person, and I think someone is tied here. Don't know why." Norie sighed. She didn't want to talk anymore, especially to a virtual stranger who seemed a little weird.

"It's been a long day, Wilhelmina." She turned to her suitcase and backpack.

"That's okay. I understand," she said. "I'll see you later." She began to move down the stairs. "By the way, I prefer Wil. Wilhelmina just sounds so old!"

As soon as Wil left, Norie felt suddenly heavy with fatigue. She sat down on the bed, her grief and anger overcoming her for a moment. Collapsing onto the pillow, she realized she had never felt so completely alone in her life. Her father was dead. Her mother, gone, in a way. Everything that happened the night of the accident was just a blur, and yet the guilt was overwhelmingly sharp. She knew everything started with her—her stupid art class, the stupid drawing box. Her promise to Gram. She thought she could play her father's game and win. She knew she was to blame for this whole mess. She buried her face in her pillow, oblivious to the swish of a skirt in the darkened corner of the attic.

# CHAPTER 7

It felt like she'd only been sleeping minutes when a few hours later Wil called her for dinner. The light was beginning to leave the attic, and through the tiny window she could see the onset of evening—a thin line of saffron in a periwinkle sky. There was a digital clock on the nightstand. It was 7:15 pm. She'd slept hard. The dampness of drool still on her cheek reminded her of Grandma Johanna. She made her way down the attic stairs to the washroom where she used a makeup remover pad to wipe off the remains of her eyeliner. She splashed water on her face and ran her fingers through her dark brown pixie cut. She had dyed it jet black once to be full goth, and her mother hated it. Norie would have kept dying it black if she could have, just to irritate Alice, but it was hard to do by herself and too expensive to do at a salon. In the end she decided her own colour was dark enough. Besides, fatigue and grief had left her face pale and drawn. The effect of her pallid skin against her dark brown hair was almost as gothic as the dye job.

The house was quiet and most of the lights were off. The kitchen though was bright, its fluorescent fixture emitting a low hum. From the kitchen window Norie could see a fire burning in the pit in the back yard and heard the animated voices of Dahlia, Wil and Gibson. Her mother was probably there too, saying nothing as usual. As she stepped out onto the back landing the warm, evening breezing felt good on her hot skin. It wouldn't be long, she thought, until that attic was way too hot to sleep in.

"You're awake!" Dahlia exclaimed. "Wonderful. Come join us," she said sliding along one of two hewn logs fashioned into low-lying benches around the pit. They looked rough, narrow, and hard, but there were cushions across them. Norie settled onto the end of one beside her mother. Alice didn't acknowledge her arrival. She just stared into the flames silently.

"Now we can make spiders!" Wil flitted around the firepit handing out long, metal roasting sticks and paper plates. Dahlia followed her with a plate of wieners sliced crisscross lengthways at each end so that they would curl up like spider legs in the heat of the fire as they cooked. On a nearby table were condiments and napkins.

"Would you like something to drink, Norie?" Gibson stood in front of her with a small cooler bag filled with canned beverages. "We have pop, iced tea, lemonade—"

"No. I don't want anything." Norie interrupted him without looking up from her roasting stick. Gibson nodded and stepped away.

Norie sat quietly while Dahlia and Wil talked about the tearoom and the lighthouse. Although they live in Burren Bay year-round, this was the tearoom's fourth summer in operation, and they were excited to grow the business into a summer destination for Island tourists. The museum was relatively new to them though, having only acquired the contract to operate it last summer from the *Friends of the Burren Bay Lighthouse* committee. It was not in bad condition, requiring a few repairs, but it was set up with historic furniture and artifacts to represent the period in which the lighthouse first operated. A second smaller building that originally held the foghorn was currently off limits to everyone. There were plans to eventually reopen it but that was in the future when more funds became available. The whole venture was a lot to manage but Gibson and some of his buddies were going to be helping with setup and repairs of the museum. Dahlia was, she said, grateful for Alice and Norie's help. Norie listened as she rotated her roasting stick over the fire. She perched the stick on the edge of the fire pit ring in a spot where the coals were almost white and watched the cut ends of the wiener on her stick curl back, darken and burn in the fire.

"Whoa!" Gibson whisked Norie's stick out of the pit, blowing on the wiener to put out the fire, then sliding it onto a paper plate. "That was just about ready to fall off! I think it's ready though." He smiled and handed her the plate. Norie did not smile back.

"So Norie," Dahlia began. "I understand you will be starting grade 10 in the fall. Any idea what courses you're taking?"

"The regular stuff," she said. Course selection had already taken place at school before the accident. "English lit, math, geography, one of the sciences. I can't remember which one." And Visual Arts 200 and 245. She would have to transfer out of those in September. Norie just couldn't do art classes now.

"I'm going into grade 10 too, but I do all my schooling online. I'm into writing and there are a ton more courses for writing online then in regular school." Norie noticed that Wil hardly breathed when she talked. She talked fast, excitement and TMI, all at once. "And because I can go at my own pace, I've already finished everything for the year. I didn't have any exams, just major year-end assignments." She took a breath. "What about you?" What about me? Those three, simple words triggered Norie.

"I got exempted from finals too." She said in a voice dripping with sarcastic politeness. "Because my father got killed in a car accident 8 weeks ago. My mother and I almost died too, but I'm really focused on school next year." Wil's face dropped—her excitement doused by Norie's angry words.

"Norie!" Alice hadn't said anything to Norie when she joined the group around the fire—hadn't said anything meaningful to her in weeks—and now she felt like she had the right to admonish her! Norie got up from the log bench, threw the paper plate and half eaten wiener into the fire leaving it to sizzle and erupt into flames, and left the backyard. Gibson moved to follow her, but Dahlia told him to let her go, to give her some space and time. Norie made her way along the stone pathway that edged the house, through the messy front yard and out the gate. Her breathing was ragged, and her heart raced. Maybe she had been rude to Wil. Maybe her words were unkind and harsh. But her mother had no right to scold her. Not anymore. Not since Norie was forced to deal with the school on her own. Not since she had to take on the running of the house and the financial worry. Not since she was the one who had to contact Dahlia to get help. Her mother had lost her rights as a parent the minute she abdicated her responsibilities.

Norie was at the general store before she became aware of her surroundings. She didn't even remember walking down the hill from Dahlia's. She didn't have a plan for where she was going or for what she was going to do. She had stomped from the back yard of *The Jolly Pot Tearoom* and back down the road they had taken that afternoon driven by her temper. Norie stopped at the bench outside the store, a 'closed' sign hanging above it in the window. She plunked herself down and buried her face in her hands. Maybe coming here was a mistake. Maybe she should have tried to get help somewhere at home. Maybe she should have spoken to someone at the school or at the doctor's office. But she wasn't 16 yet. If someone discovered that she was taking care of her mother on her own, what could have happened to her? What would happen to her now if she went back home?

She needed to keep moving. She got up off the bench and walked the short distance to the marina and Coast Guard Station on the edge of the bay. There were only a few boats moored, and Norie imagined more would arrive as the weather improved and school let out. A man was unloading a boat at the far end of the dock having just come back in from fishing. Norie could see rods, a tackle box and pails of sloshing water. When he noticed her, he nodded and smiled. Norie nodded back and made her way to the road and up a steep hill to the upper streets of Burren Bay.

The sun was slowly setting, but there was more than enough light to make her way around the village. As it turned out, there was only one extra street up the hill above the general store. Eight houses sat neatly on the street, their backyards on the edge of the hill looking out over the bay. The view from the backyards of these houses Norie knew would be magnificent, especially on a clear evening when the sun was beginning to sink in a kaleidoscope of colour. At least half of them were seasonal homes still closed for the winter. In the windows of the lived-in houses, Norie could see lights behind sheer curtains and television screens with the flashing of images of evening programming. Norie found another steep street that descended between the houses, intersecting the main street between the inn and the store. That's when she noticed, for the first time, the mural painted on a side wall of the store.

It was a painting of a lighthouse—the Burren Bay Lighthouse she assumed. It was huge, taking up most of the side wall of the building. It depicted a square, tall tower of white clapboard with red wooden trim and an attached house of the same colour and style. Around the lighthouse was a flat expanse of rock reaching back to the forest and on to the water's edge. It seemed to be a recent painting, maybe a few years old. The paint colours were still vibrant with little to no peeling or grime buildup. To paint on such a large scale always impressed Norie, and she wondered how it was done. Did the artist sketch it on the wall before painting? She couldn't see any signs of a scale underlying the paint. Maybe they projected an image onto the wall somehow. She stepped backwards to the edge of the road to get a better look of the whole painting. Who was this artist? Young? Old? She saw in the lower right-hand corner of the mural the name *Cornelia* written out in a fancy script but couldn't make out the last name in the dim light and the shadows of the plants growing wild along the bottom of the wall. She moved closer to the building for a better look but lost her footing on the uneven ground littered with stones. She slammed up against the mural on her left side grabbing at the air, trying not to fall. The shoulder and elbow she had injured in the accident took the brunt of the impact, and she had to bend over, taking deep breaths until the pain subsided. Natural consequences, she thought. Her artistic obsession had gotten her into trouble again. She stood up and pushed herself away from the mural. Limping onto the road, she turned and headed back toward the tearoom.

Movement to the right along the shoreline caught her attention. She was surprised to see a figure walking along the stony beach in the opposite direction of the marina. Norie hadn't seen anyone except the fisherman since she'd left Dahlia's. The girl, merely a shadow now as the sun sank lower into the horizon, flitted in and out of view as she moved between the trees. Norie watched her disappear into the dense cedar along the shoreline. Maybe there was a cottage nearby that she couldn't see from the road.

"There you are. Are you okay?" Wil was walking toward her on the road to the tearoom. "I was a little worried, so I came to make sure you were alright."

"I'm fine." Wil fell into step beside her.

"My mom said she thought I should give you some space. I'm sorry about what I said back there, at the fire. I just wasn't thinking and sometimes I speak before I think and—"

"Wil!" Norie interrupted her apology. "I'm fine. It's fine. Really. I'm just tired and I don't feel like talking about it." Wil nodded and fell silent.

The two girls didn't speak again until Wil said goodnight to Norie. As she lay in the murkiness of the attic bedroom, Norie felt the weight of her situation. Her arms lay heavy and limp at her sides, her wounded muscles and tissues hot and swollen with despair. Grief pressed into her chest until she almost couldn't breathe. She gulped silently for air, desperate to refill her lungs. She couldn't do it alone. Couldn't take care of her mother and herself at the same time. There was no going back home now.

# CHAPTER 8

*Burren Bay, August 1892*

Oonagh pushed through the dense tree line, falling to her knees at the edge of the black rock surrounding the lighthouse. Her hands and face were cut and scratched, and the long skirt of her nightdress did nothing to protect her knees from the sharpness of the limestone. Oonagh coughed as grey, acrid smoke meandered its way across the Burren. It swallowed everything in its path, settling like a thick fog over the rugged rock and obscuring deep crevices, petrified tree roots and low-lying juniper bushes. It brushed against her cheeks and crawled into her mouth and lungs. They rattled and wheezed as she gulped for air. She closed her eyes and tried to relax, willing her lungs to take air in and push it out. Everyone got it wrong. Everyone thought lung sickness meant you couldn't breathe in fresh air. It really meant you couldn't breathe out—couldn't empty your lungs to take that next breath. It was like drowning dry.

The foghorn blew. The lighthouse was indiscernible from where she knelt on the hard ground, but the long moan from the horn helped her get her bearings. She opened her eyes and stared into the space where she knew the lighthouse sat. That was her goal. The lighthouse. Her bedroom. The tin. The stones. Oonagh ripped off the sleeve of her nightdress which had already been torn by the trees and held the cloth over her mouth and nose. She pushed up from the ground and staggered forward, her right arm stretched outward in front of her, her feet feeling the path through her old, rotting *pampooties*. The worn rawhide slippers did little to protect her feet from the jabbing of stones and twigs. They would probably know she was gone by now. Mrs. Aubrey at the inn regularly checked on her and would have raised the alarm. Da told her to stay put. He told her that the lighthouse was safe from the fire, but that the smoke was a danger to her now. Still, she couldn't leave without the stones. She couldn't be evacuated to the mainland without them.

The fire had been detected eight days ago. It may have started long before that, but no one knew. It was on a small spit of well-treed land off the west shore of the Island, but the smoke was a danger to the ships passing through the straight. Her father and brothers were taking shifts keeping the light shining and the foghorn blowing to warn any ships in the area. The horn blew again. She veered a little more to her left as she followed the sound. Finally, through the smoke she saw the back wall of the lighthouse. She made her way around to the porch and let herself in through the kitchen door. She closed it behind her and leaned against it for a few minutes, collecting herself and taking breaths without the cloth in front of her face. Inside she could still smell the smoke and see a slight haze in the air. The old building was not sealed tightly against wind or smoke, but the air was much cleaner inside. She noticed dried food on plates in the sink and in the frying pan on the wood stove. The cream had been left out and was now soured. The men had been taking care of themselves and their strength was not in women's work. She couldn't worry about the state of the kitchen now. She had to accomplish her goal.

She moved through the kitchen to the dining room and onto the stairs to the upper bedrooms where she and her brothers slept. Her father on their first days at the lighthouse had commandeered the study and set up a cot in there. She took the smallest of the bedrooms while her three brothers bunked in the second bedroom together. The wooden stairs were steep, like a ladder moving up into the lower levels of the light tower. Afraid of tripping and falling, she gathered her nightdress into her left hand and hauled herself up the stairs with her right hand on the rail. She stopped three times to cough and clear her throat and lungs. The coughing and the climb exhausted her, and on the top step she leaned forward, struggling to breathe. When she calmed, she climbed the last step to the second floor. The haze from the smoke was a little thicker on this floor, although still better than the outdoors. She moved to her bedroom, to the dresser in the far corner. In the bottom drawer she pulled out a can with bright red letters that read Tetley Tea. The lid had bright yellow and red edging with a picture of an elephant's head stamped in the middle. Ceylon black tea imported from India. She removed the lid and checked inside. The scent of the tea still lingered along with the pungent odour of charcoal and tanned leather. She could see the pouch containing the stones at the bottom of the can and breathed a sigh of relief. She replaced the lid, thankful that she had the tin in her hands again.

Oonagh moved quickly out of the bedroom and carefully negotiated the stairs back down to the ground floor. She felt a fleeting moment of anger thinking of the cleanup she would have to do when the fire was over, and she was back in the lighthouse. But for now, she needed to get back to the inn, out of the smoke. She wet the cloth she had been holding over her face in a pail of water on the counter and made her way out of the kitchen into the haze.

The horn blew again as if announcing her departure. She moved carefully around the building and back toward the pathway to the village. She was giddy now, and a little lightheaded as she made her way across the stone pavement. Her eyes were burning, and she had to make frequent stops to double over and cough. In her weakened state she did not move carefully anymore. She found every sharp stone with the arches of her feet and tripped over the plant cover that grew along the rocks. Suddenly she stepped into a small crevice and felt her ankle turn. She lost her grip on the tea tin, and it flew forward tumbling into a much larger crevice ahead of her. She screamed, not from the pain pulsing up from her foot to her hip, but from fear of losing the stones when she was so close to safety. She tried to pull her ankle out of the crevice, but it was held fast by vines and twigs jammed into the crack.

No, no, no. This couldn't be happening. In her fall, the wet cloth she had been holding over her mouth and nose fell into a pile of dirt and leaves. The pain made her gasp and then cough. She wiggled her foot through the pain and finally released it. She began crawling on her belly across the rock where the smoke was thinner toward the crack where the tea tin fell. She stopped a few feet from the crevice when she could go no further, only able to lie gasping for air in between fits of coughing. Within seconds she stopped struggling.

As she laid there, Oonagh imagined she was lying in the soft mosses that covered the Burren in spring. She could smell the sweet scent of flowers she picked for Nan when she was a young girl, running through the rocky meadows through flora and fauna. She thought she saw her mother walking towards her, her long red hair floating loosely around her shoulders. Just steps away Oonagh reached out towards her. Her mother smiled and took her hand in cool, soft fingers.

"It's time Oonagh. I've come to get you."

"Mam, I've missed you."

"And I you," her mother answered, in the singsong voice Oonagh loved and missed terribly. "Come my little treasure..."

Hours later, when her brother found her, Oonagh lay on the hard ground, her body twisted and her head settled awkwardly on the rocky surface, the warning sob of the foghorn blaring over Burren Bay.

# CHAPTER 9

Norie awoke early the next morning after an unsettled sleep. Her waking memory was crammed with disjointed images of bent steel and broken glass, and the smell of gasoline and burning skin. She glanced at Wil sound asleep on the cot just a few feet from hers. In no mood for more apologies, prying questions and misplaced pity, she quietly dressed in shorts and a tank top and made her way from the hot, stuffy attic room. The cottage was bathed in predawn darkness except for a sliver of light coming from under the kitchen door. She could make out the sounds of pots and pans settling on the stove and a kettle on the verge of whistling. She could hear voices as well, indistinct conversation and laughter between a man and a woman. Gibson and Dahlia. Norie made her way to the front door through the main area of the tearoom and out into the morning dew. Aside from a very slight breeze, the morning was still and warm even though the sun had not yet fully risen.

She could make out her surroundings in the faint light gathering on the eastern horizon. She spotted a rough, hand-made sign simply stating *Lighthouse* with an arrow below the text. She followed it down a well-worn footpath away from the tearoom, leading to the lighthouse just beyond a small, forested area. As she walked into the shadow of the trees, she stumbled over loose rocks and vines lacing their way across the ground, masking the crevices in the limestone pavement. In the warmth of the attic, she had opted for flip-flops instead of her heavy boots. She was beginning to regret her decision. The pathway disappeared in the darkness, and she found herself in a thick copse of trees standing tightly together with their branches entangled, as if protecting what lay beyond.

As she pushed through the dense line of cedar, she found herself standing on a wide, low cliff looking out over Burren Bay. The noise of the water crashing onto the rocky shore below was loud, so much louder than it had been only a couple of feet back among the trees. The spray of the waves as they collided with the limestone shoreline dampened her face and arms. The coolness soothed the fresh scratches the branches and scale leaves of the cedars had etched in her white skin. Norie could see northward to where the bay widened and opened into a gaping mouth, swallowing the frigid waters of the North Channel.

The lighthouse sat a short distance from the edge of the cliff with the old foghorn building situated beyond it. It was the same lighthouse as the one in the mural she had seen the night before. The same but different as its age and condition were not accurate in the painting. This lighthouse was an old building, its paint cracked and peeling. The windows—there were few—were covered by shutters askew on their hinges. A well-worn tarp had probably spent the winter draped across the southeast corner. It flapped loosely in the wind, its edges raw and sinewy. The light itself was installed in a lantern room at the top of the square, white wooden tower trimmed in red. Surrounding the tower was a single-story white building, also trimmed in red. She began to move forward toward the building as the sun ascended above the horizon shining on the lighthouse and illuminating the morning mist swirling around its base. Beyond the lighthouse, the shoreline fell like great steps to the water's edge. Waves lapped aggressively up onto the rock pavement there.

Norie looked down as she wandered along the cliff's edge, careful to step around carpets of lichen and moss and over the small, loose stones that littered the surface. Large cracks in the flat, blackened pavement had also formed from the thousands of years of the freeze and thaw cycle. In some places the scars in the rocks were a couple of feet wide. She could see down into them to where plants and grasses attempted to take hold and grow in thin soil and debris blown in over time. She stopped, gazing into a particularly deep and wide crevice. Staring down made her dizzy, but she was unable to look away. It ran the whole width of a huge block, right to the water's edge. Water flowed in and out at the bottom creating a hollow thud, like drumming on an empty plastic container. The water rushed in and then just as quickly back out of the crevice, matching the rhythm of the waves. It was hypnotic.

As she peered into the shallowest point in the crack, about a foot or so down, she noticed something shiny—a metal object reflecting the small ray of sunlight, shining into this space at exactly this time of day when the sun was just over the horizon. It looked like a box or can.

"They're called grikes and clints."

Norie closed her eyes and sighed. Apparently, she had not left the attic room as quietly as she thought. She turned to face Wil.

"What?" Norie asked.

"The cracks and rock chunks are called grikes and clints. They make up the alvar pavement or this whole rocky surface here." She waved her hands around her indicating the land they were on. "The grikes and clints are formed by water erosion. When the ice cap—"

"It's okay," Norie interrupted, hands raised defensively, "I don't need to know."

"They're kind of beautiful though, aren't they?" Wil crouched down beside the grike that Norie had been peering into and watched the water flow in and back out onto itself. "Scary, but beautiful."

Norie agreed silently.

"So, my mom told me to tell you that breakfast is ready. She expects all of us to sit down to eat together. It's this thing about creating a circle of belonging."

"Belonging to what?" Norie asked as she knelt beside the crevice and reached in to grab the object. Something soft brushed across her skin, like fingertips gently pushing her hand toward the object. She pulled back quickly, thinking a spider had crawled across her hand. She could see nothing. She reached in again and pulled out the object.

"I guess to us." Wil leaned over Norie's shoulder, gazing into the crack, into Norie's hand. "What do you have there?"

"I don't know. I just saw something shiny," she replied, turning the object over in her hands. It was an old square tin—its stamped labels badly weathered, and the lid rusted on.

"It's a tea tin I bet," Wil said, "Mom has a few old tins in the teapot museum. That's how people bought stuff back in the day. Kept stuff fresh and dry." Norie tried prying off the lid, but it wouldn't budge. She shook the tin and could hear something banging around inside. "Let's take it back to the house. I bet my mom could take the lid off. She's a pro with a squirt of cooking spray!"

"It's okay," Norie hugged the can to her body. "I'll try later myself."

When they got back to the tearoom, she took a few minutes

to run up to the bedroom and tuck the can into her backpack. She washed her hands and made her way back to the kitchen. In the hallway Norie noticed a small, framed sketch hanging beside a piece of macramé art and a calendar that was still showing August of the previous year. The frame looked handmade, roughly cut and aged with patina. The sketch was titled, *Burren Bay*, but it didn't really look like the bay Norie had just seen. The bay in the sketch was much bigger. The waters around it appeared to extend out toward the horizon as if there were no land beyond, as if the bay opened to the ocean. Norie liked the soft roughness of the sketch—quick charcoal lines over layers of soft and dark tones. This was the medium she intended to use in her final assignment in art class. But it never happened. She noticed initials in the corner of the sketch: *O.M.* Whoever *O.M.* was, they had a way with charcoal. At that moment Norie was unexpectedly overcome with the heaviness of loss—her knees buckled, and she almost fell to the floor. She grabbed at the corner of the wall to steady herself taking deep breaths, trying to overcome the fear of losing control of her body. When she was finally able to stand on her own, she continued toward the kitchen, confused by the incident but desperate to regain normalcy. That had never happened before. Losing control was frightening.

As she entered the room, she spotted her mother sitting in the same spot she had sat in the day before. It struck her that this was the first morning since Alice came home from the hospital that she didn't have to help her mother get up and get ready. Norie hadn't given her mother her night or morning medications. She hadn't applied cream and bandages to her wounds. For the first time in weeks, Norie had only herself to think about. She was both relieved and unsettled. Her mother smiled at her when their gaze met, but her lips were tight and her eyes dark. Norie looked away and took a seat beside Wil on the opposite side of the table.

Gibson sat between Wil and Dahlia.

"Welcome to breakfast!" Dahlia greeted her as she placed a heaping plate of scones on the table among pots of homemade jams and jellies. She sat down and reached her hands out to Norie's mother and Gibson. "Let's join hands for the morning blessing." Norie watched as Alice tentatively took Dahlia's left hand while Gibson took Dahlia's right. Beside her Wil stretched out her hand, but Norie ignored it, bowing her head instead. Wil looked down as well, in disappointment, until Gibson grabbed her other hand and squeezed it. Norie looked away in embarrassment.

"This is a special Celtic prayer—a protective prayer called a *caim*. It's quite beautiful," Dahlia said and then she recited,

"Circle us, keep hope within, and despair without.
Circle us, keep peace within, and worry without.
Circle us, keep love within, and hatred without.
Circle us, keep courage within, and fear without.
Circle us, keep light within, and darkness without."

With that the prayer was over. "Help yourself. Wilhelmina, pour the tea, would you love?" Wil deftly managed the large porcelain pot covered in a pink and green crocheted cosy, pouring into each of their tea cups without spilling so much as a drop. "Now that you're here, Norie, I have something to give the two of you."

"That's not necessary, Dahlia. You have given us a place to stay, you don't need to give gifts too." Norie's mother looked mortified.

"It's not that kind of gift my friend. I want you two to use your time here to heal." Oh brother, thought Norie, here it comes. "Alice, I have this for you." She reached under the table to retrieve something from a gift bag on the floor. "I know you journaled a lot when we were in university and we both know that was helpful during difficult times." Norie wondered what she meant. Dahlia's voice softened. "Here." She handed Alice a small journal and pen. "I think it's worth trying. To get your thoughts down in writing. To work through things...from my hands to yours." Alice took the journal and pen with shaking hands. Norie lowered her eyes, embarrassed by the sentimental exchange between the two old friends, uneasy about the past Dahlia spoke about.

"And for you Miss Norie, I have something for the young artist." No, no, no, screamed Norie silently. Dahlia leaned toward her, a sketchbook and package of pencils in hand. "I know you are a student of art and thought art may be the way for you to work through things. From my hands to yours." Norie thought she was going to throw up. This time it was her hands shaking as she took the sketchbook and pencils with only a nod.

Dahlia, Gibson, and Wil chatted happily as they ate breakfast. Her mother answered questions when asked. Norie ignored the gift and tried to follow the conversation. Gibson was a truck driver for Island Transport and would be coming and going throughout the summer. He and Dahlia met a few years ago and grew closer over time. Last summer they made it official and got married right on the cliffs surrounding the lighthouse. Alice asked about the plans for the tearoom and museum. After cleaning the tearoom, setting up Dahlia's collection of teapots in the teapot museum, and cleaning the lighthouse, most of the work would revolve around running the tearoom and lighthouse museum.

Norie tried to concentrate on what was being said but her gaze kept returning to the empty sketchbook. It was as if the sketchbook she left on the bus had found its way back to her like some weird haunting. Grandma Johanna had told Norie that she came from a long line of artists—musicians, painters, writers, and dancers all free to express their creativity, part of a growing family tree both hardy and verdant. But the accident, her father's betrayal and death, had broken Norie. Now she was a fractured branch that would not mend. She turned away from the sketchbook.

"Wilhelmina, you and Norie are going to start in the lighthouse museum. Just clean and tidy for now and when that's done, you can start sorting through that cache of things we found in the old storeroom." Wil, thrilled at the idea of setting up, high-fived her mother.

"I will see who I can get to come re-shingle the roof and repair the interior spaces before we get too far into the season," added Gibson leaning in to kiss Dahlia on the cheek. "I've got to get to work. I will see you all later." He squeezed Wil's shoulder as he moved behind her chair, nodding to Alice and Norie on his way out of the kitchen. Norie ignored him. Again.

While it sounded easy enough, cleaning and tidying the lighthouse museum was hot and exhausting work. It was a very old building, sitting in a very damp environment that had been closed-up since the summer before. The tarp Norie had seen flapping loosely in the wind that morning had done its job, but not until rain and weather had already caused a mess in one bedroom and a storage room that would be closed to the public until they were repaired. Norie discovered by the end of her first week that things moved very slowly on the Island. She was sore and exhausted by the time the cleaning and set up was done. She and Wil spent long hours washing floors and walls, dusting furniture and artifacts, and posting signage telling interesting, historical information about each room. Two people from the *Friends of the Burren Bay Lighthouse*, a local historical preservation group, came early in the week and were pleased with their progress. Other than them, Dahlia, Wil, Gibson, and her mother, Norie saw very few other people during that week.

The museum, however, did hold a certain fascination for her. It was a four-room facility on the main floor of the lighthouse with artifacts on display showing life at the lighthouse back in the late

1800s. The kitchen, dining room and parlour were all set up with collections of furniture showing how people lived. A back room of the museum, originally a bedroom, represented the nautical history of the area, and there was a large table and chairs that Norie assumed were for research. Upstairs on the second floor were two bedrooms. One was set up like a child's room with a crib, toys and clothing on display, and the other they called the parents' room would have an old bed, wash basin, and dresser in it once the repairs were finished. A further staircase, a steep ladder-like staircase, went up to the light room. From its vantage point, you could see beyond the bay, almost to the shore across the North Channel.

The museum entrance was through a small closed-in porch leading into the kitchen. It was just inside the porch, beside the kitchen door that Norie and Wil set up a counter displaying pamphlets about other lighthouses and museums on the Island, advertisements for various resorts and restaurants, and flyers announcing upcoming activities in the local townships. One of the pamphlets was about the Burren Bay Lighthouse—its history, hours of operation, and entrance fees.

"Read this," said Wil. "You'll have to give little tours and answer questions when visitors are here, and this explains everything." Norie recognized the name of the author of the pamphlet as one of the women from the *Friends of the Burren Bay Lighthouse* she met during the clean-up. She opened the pamphlet and began to read, trying to memorize details set out on the timeline. She learned that when Manitoulin Island was being colonized in the late 1800s, many of the surveyors named towns and bays after their hometowns in Europe and Great Britain. Burren Bay was named after the Burren in County Clare, Ireland. The sketch she had seen earlier in Dahlia's house made sense now. Maybe *O.M.* was the surveyor who came to Manitoulin Island. The charcoal sketch was probably the original Burren Bay on the coast of Ireland. Norie knew nothing about Ireland, except what Grandma Johanna told her. Until now, frankly, she hadn't any interest in it.

"I think we're done," Wil sat back on her stool. "Tomorrow is the fun part. I love going through stuff that we find here. You never know what you're going to discover." Norie remembered the tin can she had discovered in the crevice on the cliff days before. She had a sudden urge to know what was in the can, to make her own discovery. But she wanted to do it alone. She was used to being alone.

"Mom wants me to go into the village to the store to pick up some baking supplies she ordered. Do you want to come with me?"

"Maybe next time," Norie said. "I'm pretty tired." She was tired, but she was more interested in exploring the can without Wil stuck to her the whole time.

"Oh, okay. I guess I'll see you later," said Wil. Norie felt guilty, but only a little.

She made her way back to the tearoom, where Dahlia was busy weeding and planting, while her mother sat on a bench, staring out over the bay. She slipped into the house and up to her bedroom. She took the can out of her backpack, turning it over in her hands. Although weather beaten, she could see that the lid of the can had been trimmed in gold and red with the picture of an elephant in the centre, clasping a crate in its trunk. Holding it under the lamp light, she could just make out the larger red letters spelling T-E-?-?-E-Y. Maybe TEA-something? Wil had said she thought it was a tea tin.

*Tetley*! Norie realized. It was a tea tin. A *Tetley* tea tin! The sides of the tin were almost bare of any paint at all. Again, she tried to pull off the lid, but it was rusted shut. She recalled Wil's comment about her mother doing all sorts of stuff with cooking spray.

Norie quietly made her way to the kitchen. Her mother and Dahlia were still outside working in the flower beds, so she was able to search the kitchen without interruption. She found a can of cooking spray in a cupboard alongside a variety of oils and vinegars. She also grabbed a scouring pad from under the sink and a wad of paper towels before she made her way back up to her room, where she set to work rubbing and scraping the rust off the lid of the can. The spray oil was effective as a cleaner and Norie could see the labelling a little clearer. It was a tea tin, but she had no idea how old it was. The words Indian Ceylon appeared faint on the lid. Finally, after she scraped as much rust off as possible and cleaned and oiled the seam where the lid and can met, Norie gave a couple of hard pulls and felt the lid move. A few more wiggles released the lid completely along with flakes of rust and paint and a stale odour that had been trapped inside for who knows how long. Norie thought she heard movement downstairs and froze, listening, but she couldn't hear any sound. She glanced around the attic room, unable to shake the feeling of being watched. Nothing moved, not even with the tiny breeze blowing through the window. Norie returned her attention to the tea tin and gazed into the can. A surprisingly pleasant woody smell of oil and earth met her nostrils, and a flash of memory flooded her brain—the memory of the first time she peered into Grandma Johanna's art box. The tin was as smooth inside as the wood of the antique box was, the rust of weather not yet having made its way into the interior of the can. At the bottom, among black dust and crumbles, sat four or five, narrow pieces of charcoal, a feather, and a tube of what looked like leather, tightly rolled and bound by twine. It was an artist's box too. She was sure of that. She had no idea how old it was, where it was from or to whom it belonged, but she instantly felt as if this was a sacred tin that needed her protection. She lost her antique art box, but she wasn't going to lose this one. Again, she glanced up from the can unable to shake the feeling of being watched.

Turning her attention back she saw tucked in amongst these

items a small pouch made of soft leather, smudged with charcoal dust. This too reminded her of her grandmother's art box with its reddish gold colouring and warm smooth surface. Small, tight stitches kept the edges of the pouch sealed. A thin fringe of leather strips hung from the bottom of the pouch—again a memory flash of a leather thong, cascading through Gram's frail fingers. There were beads sewn onto the front of the pouch, but the thread there was brittle, and many of the beads had fallen off into the tin. The opening of the pouch was tightly gathered by a long, leather thong, but Norie managed to pry it open. Nestled inside were three stones. They looked like the rocks she saw scattered around the lighthouse, pointy and multifaceted like arrow heads or diamonds. They were as light as bone and warm in her hand. A little family of stones. A sudden knock on the door startled her.

"Norie? Can I come up to get some of the boxes out of the corner?" It was Gibson standing at the bottom of the stairs. Norie replaced the lid and returned the tin to her backpack.

"Sure," she responded, stuffing the pouch and stones into her pocket. She watched Gibson's head appear out of the opening for the attic stairs. He smiled and nodded as he moved toward the pile of boxes and lifted several of the smaller ones at once. He turned toward where Norie sat on the cot and smiled.

"So how was your first week in the lighthouse?" Norie picked up her backpack busying herself with organizing objects that didn't need organizing.

"It was fine."

"Do you think you will enjoy working there?"

"Hard to tell right now."

The awkwardness of the conversation was not lost on Gibson, and Norie was acutely aware of it. He stood in the silence until finally he gave up and moved toward the stairs. Gibson quickly exited the attic and Norie could hear his footsteps on the lower staircase to the basement. She quickly gathered up the cooking spray, scouring pad and dirty paper towels and returned them to the kitchen. She went back to the attic intent on exploring the contents of the can and returning the small pouch. She was startled again, but this time by the slamming of the front screen door announcing Wil's return. A moment later Wil stuck her head into the attic space.

"Mom says it's our job to make the salad for dinner." She turned and left the room without another word.

Norie sighed, dusted the dirt from the tin off her cot and headed downstairs.

# CHAPTER 10

Dishes, Norie discovered, were also a part of her duties at Dahlia's. Well, not just her duties, Wil's as well. The two girls moved around the kitchen silently that night. Wil washed and Norie dried, placing the dishes on the table until she learned where everything went. They didn't talk. The silence was broken only by the squeak of the hot water tap, the running water, and the clinking of the dishes. She knew Wil was still upset that she didn't join her to go to the village. Norie didn't mind the silence. It gave her time to look around the kitchen, to think. She gazed out the open window toward the street that led to the village, to where Alice and Dahlia were strolling. She watched as Dahlia took her mother's arm in her own, supporting her as they walked along. Her mother was so needy it almost sickened Norie. A tiny bird landed on the windowsill and pecked at crumbs that appeared to be sprinkled in a line along the whole length of the sill. Weird way to feed the birds, she thought. The little bird looked at Norie for a second then picked up one of the larger crumbs and flew away, her wing brushing the chime hanging mid-window.

Turning away, she noticed a shelf on the far wall of the kitchen between the table and the back door. It was hung chest high with an ornate mirror hanging on the wall above it. At first Norie thought it was just a random shelf. A spot to dump things like keys or mail as you came through the door. She approached it and gazed into the mirror for a moment at the pale fatigue of her face. God, she looked like her father. It was a little haunting to notice now that he was gone. Her dark hair, Irish hair Grandma Johanna called it, fell around the nape of her neck and was starting to curl around her high cheekbones, just like his unruly hair did. Her lips, thin and the palest of pink, reminded her of her father's lips. She could always tell when he was plotting and planning. His lips would be drawn tight and his jawline tense. Her eyes, though, were not his. Her eyes, almond shaped with hazel irises surrounded by amber rings, belonged to her mother. And to Grandma Johanna.

She sighed and looked more closely at the long and narrow shelf. On it were a strange collection of items: a photo of Dahlia and Gibson's wedding, a photo of Wil, Dahlia and a man taken several years earlier, another photo of the bay tucked behind it, a candle, some dried flowers, and a small bowl of what looked to be gems and unusual stones.

"That's my mother's altar. Well, I guess it's really a family altar." Wil spoke from the kitchen sink.

"Altar? Like in a church?"

"No. Well, maybe yes. I guess it's a little like a church altar. It's a space where you can put important, special things to help you focus on them," Wil answered. "We try to change some of the stuff every so often." She dried her hands and moved to where Norie was standing. "That photo is always there though. That's my mom and dad and me when I was about 5 years old."

"I thought you said your father left you?"

"He did...the year after this picture was taken." Wil gazed at the picture. "But we don't hate him, you know. He was just a broken man. We don't want him back, but we still want him to find happiness and peace. He does belong to us after all." Wil sounded like she was reading a script for a public service announcement. Norie wasn't so sure she believed her. Sometimes people just lose the right to belong. She was sure that Gibson too, would do something to lose his right to belong on the altar. Her father did. "The candle, obviously, is to bring light into any darkness we may feel. I put the dried flowers there last summer. I thought they were pretty." Norie wondered what she would put on her altar. Not a picture of her family. Maybe a picture of Grandma Johanna. She couldn't think of another thing. Wil drifted back to the counter then added, "You can add something if you want."

"Can I take something?"

"Like what?"

"This photo of the bay." Norie was still intrigued by the bay she had seen the day after she arrived and how it compared to the bay in the charcoal sketch in the hallway. She picked up the photo in her free hand and looked more closely at it. It captured the whole bay from the same spot she saw it that first morning. Only the corner of the lighthouse was visible, while the whole bay from shore to shore could be seen.

"I guess so," Wil said, "If you need it, you need it, right?"

"I don't need it," said Norie, with an edge to her voice that surprised her. She put the photo back and finished drying the dish in her hand. A light breeze rippled across the wind chime and blew a few of the crumbs off the windowsill. Norie stuck her hand in her pocket, feeling for the pouch of stones, rubbing her thumb over the few remaining beads, trying to relax.

"Whatever," said Wil pulling the plug on the sink. "Let's put the dishes away now."

The next day dawned hot and humid. Norie and Wil found themselves crowded into a tiny storage room under the lighthouse staircase, smelling strongly of damp cardboard and mildew. A couple of the boxes had to be immediately thrown away due to water damage and Dahlia's fear of mould. The rest were filled with a variety of things, some important to the lighthouse's history: receipts for supplies from the last few years the lighthouse and foghorn station were in operation, accounting ledgers, and brief duty logs. Some of the paperwork was from past managers of the museum before Dahlia and Wil took over. The girls sorted into two piles—keepers and garbage. Any documents that were not lighthouse related were tossed into the garbage pile, while anything having to do with the lighthouse, even if it was from more recent years, was kept. Norie searched through the contents of an old chocolate box. It had several newspaper clippings concerning the lighthouse. Most of them were from the last thirty years, but there was an old black and white photo in the collection. It was the lighthouse in its early days with what looked like the entire town all in their Sunday best gathered around it. The people were dressed in old fashioned dresses and suits, large fancy hats and one woman carried a parasol. The photo was old and grainy, so it was difficult to make out any faces. She turned it over and on the back in handwriting was Easter Sunday 1910. Norie placed it on the keep pile along with most of the contents of the box.

On the very bottom, tucked between two sheets of tissue paper, were two charcoal sketches. They were both about the same size as the one hanging in the tearoom. One was a sketch of the bay from the same angle as the photo on Dahlia's altar in the kitchen, while the other was of the lighthouse. The lighting in the storage room was not the best so Norie got up and moved into the hallway.

"What's that?" Wil asked.

"Some old drawings." Norie could see both were signed with the same initials as the framed sketch: *O.M.* The charcoal work of the two drawings was smudged and not as clear as the one in the tearoom, but Norie guessed it was from being pressed at the bottom of the box in the damp storage area for who knows how long. The smudging gave the work a mystical quality though. It was as if she were looking at the bay and lighthouse through a veil. She glanced at Wil who sat inside the storage room looking through yet another pile of papers. She looked back to the sketches and ran her fingertips lightly around the edges of the paper. She wanted the sketches. An odd breeze blew through the hallway, giving Norie goosebumps.

"Hello!" They could hear Gibson call as he entered the lighthouse. "Just coming to see how things are going and if you have the storeroom emptied yet." He entered the hall just as Wil crawled out of the tiny closet.

"We're pretty much done sorting," Wil announced as she exited the storage closet and stood beside Norie. "Hey those are like the one Mom has hanging in the house. I wonder who made them?" Gibson glanced over Wil's shoulder at the drawings.

"Yes, I think you're right." Norie stood still, trying to decide how she could keep the drawings now that both Wil and Gibson had seen them.

"You should keep them." Wil declared. "Maybe they will inspire you." She moved away from where Norie was standing and added, "I'm starving! Let's go see if dinner is ready. Are you coming Gibson?"

"I have to take a look at what we have in the way of interior damage in here. Ray Fox needs a report so he can order materials. Tell your mother I'll be there in a couple of minutes."

Norie wrapped the sketches back in the tissue and ran after

Wil, who was already at the door of the lighthouse.

"You don't think your mom will mind if I take these?" Norie asked.

"Why would she?" Wil pushed through the screen door into the sunshine.

"What if they are worth something?" Norie asked, hurrying behind her. Wil stopped and turned to Norie.

"They're worth something to you, right? That's all that really matters." Norie didn't know what to say, so she just nodded.

When they got back to the tearoom, Norie hurried up to their bedroom and slid the two sketches in the sketchbook Dahlia had given her. She sat on her bed for a moment, breathless. She was aware of the stones in her pocket, sharp edges pressing against her hip bone even through the fabric of the pouch. The bag and bead work were fragile, but she couldn't bring herself to separate them. She stood again and reached into her pocket and pulled out the pouch emptying it into her hand. The three stones were warmer in her hand now because of her own body heat. The sound of movement in the darkest corner of the room startled Norie. She peered into the blackness. Oh God, she thought, mice. She carefully placed the stones back in the pouch, stuffed it back into her pocket, and hurried from the room.

Norie made her way to the kitchen but found it empty. She moved into the sitting area that would soon become the main tearoom when they opened on the July 1st weekend, and found her mother, sitting at the table, pen in hand, journal open in front of her, staring into space.

"Where is everyone?" Norie asked. Her mother startled and turned to look at her.

"Dahlia decided we needed a treat tonight, so she and Wil went to get take-out fish and chips. Gibson is out at the lighthouse, I think." They were the first words her mother had spoken to her in days and Norie was stunned by the faintness of her voice. It was as if she couldn't breathe in and out in the right rhythm for speaking.

"Oh," Norie replied. She slipped her hand in her pocket touching the pouch of stones. "What are you up to?" Alice closed the journal but not before Norie saw that the page was empty.

"Nothing," she said, then added, "Just thinking and writing." Another lie. Norie could feel her anger rise. She needed to escape.

"I'll be back in a bit," she said as she moved quickly to the door. She didn't hear her mother respond. She didn't expect her to.

Outside she made her way to the lighthouse path. She knew it well now, having travelled it back and forth repeatedly over the last weeks. She easily found the opening between the trees leading her to the rock pavement. The bay at this time in the late afternoon had a light she found difficult to find words for. It was simply breathtaking. She immediately thought of the little sketches she found earlier. The one of the bay must have been sketched exactly at this time of day. The artist got the shading perfectly. The light, smudged strokes of charcoal applied to the paper created the same golden glow. Norie wondered where the artist had stood. She moved along the tree line away from the lighthouse and toward a widening view of the bay. She watched the bay as she moved slowly along the cliff, about thirty feet back from the edge closer to the tree line. Suddenly, as if looking through the lens of a camera, the view of the bay she was searching for appeared. It was centred and framed exactly like the sketch. She was certain the artist had not stood on the open cliff to draw, even now on a relatively calm evening the breeze was too strong to keep an easel upright or paper from flapping on a board. She searched for a perch—a place where the artist must have sat and worked. She turned gazing into the trees, looking for places where the branches' shadows shifted, where they opened into hidden alcoves. Her eyes followed a wide crack in the pavement back toward the tree line. At some point, whether by frost heave or ice effect, a part of the pavement had broken off and was lifted out of its spot right where the trees began to grow. The trees had been forced to grow around the boulder creating the perfect sheltered seat. Norie ran to the rock throne and sat down facing out towards the bay. This was it. This was where the artist had sat, just far enough amongst the trees to be sheltered from wind. Norie pushed herself further back on the boulder and crossed her legs. There was more than enough room for a sketchbook or drawing board in front of her. The rock was warm from the sun and relatively smooth under her hands. She was gazing out over the bay, pleased that she had found the secret spot, when her mother stepped from the opening in the trees along the lighthouse path.

At first Norie moved back into the branches of the surrounding trees, not wanting her mother to see her, but then she realized she was hidden from view. She watched her mother slowly make her way to the edge of the cliff. Along the way she bent to pick the tall grasses that grew in between the crevices. Her long, thin, dark hair blew wildly as she got further from the break of the trees and closer to the edge of the rock pavement. Was her mother following her? Did she want to talk now? Well, Norie didn't want to talk. Alice should have stayed at the tearoom writing imaginary words in her journal. Her mother carefully looked over the cliff edge to where the waves crashed against the rocks. Suddenly Gibson came around the corner of the lighthouse and Alice abruptly turned, as if he had called for her. They talked briefly and then both made their way back to the trees, back to the tearoom. Gibson turned looking toward the edge of the rock, then followed her mother through the path. Norie breathed a sigh of relief. Her secret spot was still a secret. She intended to keep it that way.

# CHAPTER 11

The darkness came again. She struggled to open her eyes before it swallowed her up, but her head was pounding and every square inch of her ached. She knew if she just relaxed, she could find some relief, giving into the pain and fear. There was the familiar crackling, snapping sound in front of her. The warmth of the fire spread over her, beginning at her toes, and travelling upwards to her head. The heat intensified, and she turned her head away and opened her eyes again, finding her father's lifeless body slumped over the steering wheel. Blood was running freely from his ear and from a gash on his head. His eyes open but vacant. She tried to scream but was choked by the increasing smoke and the heat of the flames.

Norie awoke sitting straight up in bed, her breath ragged and tears streaming down her cheeks. Wil was kneeling beside her, concern written on her face.

"Norie, are you okay? Do you want me to go get your mother?"

"No!" Norie snapped. "No, just give me a minute." She took

deep breaths, squeezing her eyes shut tightly, trying to erase the images from her mind.

Norie opened her eyes, remembering where she was. Remembering she was not in her old house, in her old bedroom, in her old life. Opening her eyes, letting in the dim light of the attic, blurred the images and faded the nightmare a little. She inhaled and exhaled into a normal rhythm.

"This one was bad, wasn't it?" Wil asked.

"What do you mean?"

"You dream like this every night. But this one was the worst I've seen."

"Every night?" She usually couldn't remember dreaming. The haunting in her sleep had become insidious, making her exhausted and irritable all the time. Her new way of life, she supposed. But tonight, she remembered.

"Do you want to talk about it?"

"No!" She could see by the look on Wil's face that she had responded too sharply, too emphatically.

"Well, okay then. I'm going to try to go back to sleep." Wil moved back to her cot. Norie knew she should say something, but she couldn't find the words. She lay back on her pillow and stared up at the exposed roof beams. Eventually she slipped back into a troubled sleep.

At breakfast that morning, Norie sat quietly in her spot beside the window. During the belonging circle ritual that Dahlia insisted on performing each morning, she studied the line of crumbs on the windowsill. *Circle us.* It looked fresh this morning, as if someone had replaced them in a near perfect straight line, and the birds hadn't spotted them yet. *Keep courage within.* She wanted to know but couldn't summon the energy to ask. *And fear without.* Her attention was drawn back to the table when Wil released her hand after the blessing.

"Everything is pretty much ready for the July 1st weekend," Dahlia said. "I want to go to Prosper Bay today and drop in on the artist who's displaying her work here for the month of July. I think we could all use a change of scenery."

"Well, you lovely ladies enjoy your outing. I'm off on a long haul, and I won't be back for a few days." Gibson leaned in and kissed Dahlia and hugged Wil. "Don't forget that Ray Fox will be over to the lighthouse in the next few days to start the repairs. I left his contact info in your agenda on your desk." He nodded at Norie and her mother. Her mother smiled meekly, but Norie just looked away.

"Thanks Gibson," Dahlia replied as he left the kitchen. "Drive safe and call me!"

Within the hour the four of them were crammed into Dahlia's small two door car, Wil and Norie in the back seat and Alice in the front passenger seat. At first Norie was sure her mother wasn't going to get in the car. From the back seat, she could see Dahlia speaking to her, their heads close, almost touching and Dahlia's hand gently rubbing Alice's arm. Eventually they both got in, although her mother never really relaxed throughout the whole ride. She sat erect and still, as if her body was unwilling to lean fluidly with the car making its way down the winding highway.

Prosper Bay was half an hour from Burren Bay. It was a much bigger community boasting a full-sized grocery store, drugstore, a library, and other shops lining the main street. Dahlia made her way towards the marina where Norie could see sail boats, smaller yachts and a large fishing tug moored at the docks. They parked outside a large, old building that sat right at the shore of the bay just beyond the marina. The lower floor housed various businesses, while the upper level had three artists' studios. Nell Gallagher's studio was at the rear of the building facing out over the water. Norie glanced around at the many paintings hanging on the walls. A large easel, a work in progress perched on it, sat in the far corner of the room with pots of paint and thinner sitting on tables nearby. The artist sat on a low stool thumbing through sketchbooks stacked beside her. From her crouched position, she appeared to be wrapped in multi-layered pieces of bright purple, yellow and green cloth. She looked up through small round glasses perched on the end of her nose as the visitors wound their way towards her.

"Dahlia, I was wondering if you would have time to visit. I was sure you'd be on your front porch with Wil and Gibson sipping lemonade in this unbearable heat."

"That would be lovely, but impossible! Opening day is just a week away! I've come to talk about what you're going to bring to the tearoom," said Dahlia.

"Are these the friends you told me about who are staying with you?" Nell stood up to greet them, allowing the rainbow layers of cloth to fall into place. She was tall and slim, her long thin neck adding to the illusion of height. Her hair was piled up into a high knot on the very top of her head, instantly reminding Norie of a fancy layer cake topper she had seen on a cooking show.

"Yes, they are. This is my good friend Alice Lynch and her daughter Norie. They're visiting with me for the summer, helping at the tearoom and museum." Norie nodded while her mother stood awkwardly in silence off to the side gazing out at the bay.

"Can Norie and I just look around while you and Mom talk?" asked Wil.

"Of course. We shouldn't be long. Just be careful of the open jars of turpentine." Wil grabbed Norie's hand and pulled her away to the back of the studio. It was the perfect space for creating art, with huge windows allowing for plenty of natural light. Part of the studio was set up as a gallery, while the rest was divided into work and office spaces, as well as storage. She followed Wil to the gallery area. It became quickly apparent that Nell's preferred subjects were old buildings, waterfalls, and dilapidated farms. Leaning up against a desk were six or seven framed paintings that were waiting to be hung. The whole stack of paintings was of lighthouses the same colour and style as the one at Burren Bay. Norie flipped through them until she found herself looking at a familiar lighthouse sitting on a cliff looking out over the water. She could almost hear the noise of the waves crashing onto the rocky shore and feel the spray of water on her face. This was also the same lighthouse in the mural on the wall of the store in the village. In the corner of the painting was the artist's signature: *Cornelia Gallagher.* Nell Gallagher was the same artist who painted the mural on the general store in Burren Bay.

"You found my lighthouse collection. I love lighthouses, don't you?" Nell was now standing beside her as she scanned the lighthouse pictures. "These are the pictures I am bringing to display at the *Jolly Pot*. Do you like them?" Norie nodded. "Dahlia tells me you are quite the young artist yourself." Norie cringed, anticipating the questions, the prodding.

"I don't do much art right now," she said. Not anymore. She shoved her hands in her pocket, her fingertips brushing the beads on the pouch of stones.

"Maybe you can help me when I hang these at the tearoom. I could sure use another set of hands." Norie stared at the paintings and nodded mutely. Wil wandered up to them.

"Mom says it's time to go."

"I have something for the two of you." Nell moved to a box of smaller, unframed prints, thumbing through until she found two identical copies of the painting of the Burren Bay Lighthouse. She gave them to Wil and Norie.

"A gift," she said as she handed one to each girl. She held Norie's gaze for a few seconds longer.

"Thanks." Norie tried to keep her voice calm, emotionless.

"Well, we'd better get going. We still need to have lunch and get to the grocery store. So, you'll bring your paintings Thursday?" Dahlia asked.

"That's right. I'll be out in the morning," she said. Then turning to Norie, she added, "Norie here has agreed to be my helper when I come. I hope it's okay that I steal her away for a couple of hours."

"Of course. Everything is ready to go in the museum, so the girls are pretty much finished with the setup. We have Ray Fox from Rocky Plains coming to do the repairs soon. Wil was just going to help me bake that morning anyway. Besides, Norie is the artist in this group. I'm sure she would love to help." Dahlia and Wil moved to the entrance of the studio, gathering Alice who hadn't moved from the window.

"Maybe when I bring out my stuff you could show me some of your work?"

"I don't have anything to show you," admitted Norie, simultaneously embarrassed and bitter. She swallowed the lump in her throat and grasped the bag of stones in her hand, pressing their shapes through the old cloth into her palm like shells into clay.

"Then maybe we can just talk about art." Norie nodded mutely and hurried out to catch up to everyone.

"Oh, there you are," said Wil, having turned back to get Norie, "We thought you got lost."

"I wish your mother would stop doing that!" Norie blurted out, her face red and hands clenched.

"Stop doing what," Wil asked, taken aback.

"Stop trying to get me into art again! Stop trying to get me to draw!" Norie was breathless now with anger. "I don't want anything to do with it anymore."

"My mom is just trying to help." Wil whimpered. Norie knew she was upsetting her. But she couldn't stop.

"Maybe I don't need that kind of help!" Norie stomped ahead

of Wil toward the door. Wil grabbed her arm stopping her in her tracks.

"We're both just trying to help and all you've been is rude. My mom and Gibson have welcomed you into their home, no, their livelihood. Mom's given you gifts. Babysits your mother. I've tried including you in everything we do. I've given you your space. I even wake up every night with your stupid nightmares! Remember you called us, not the other way around. You called us!" Wil ran out past Norie leaving her speechless, standing in the entrance way alone.

While Dahlia and Alice went grocery shopping, the two girls were dropped off at the *Prosper Bay Public Library* to return books and pick a few new ones to borrow for the next few weeks. Neither girl spoke to the other as they browsed the shelves, making sure to move in different directions down different aisles, carefully avoiding each other. Norie chose four mystery books from the YA collection and then spent the rest of the next hour avoiding Wil in the local history section flipping through old copies of a magazine series called *Manitoulin Island History*. One whole volume was dedicated to lighthouses and lighthouse keepers and their families.

Very little information, other than names and a few brief stories, existed of lighthouse keepers in the late 1800s. Keeper's logs, newspaper accounts, and various personal journals provided most of the information. Keepers came from all over the world. Some were looking for work after returning from war. Some were looking for a new start away from the pressures of the city. Some were looking for a place to heal. Either way, prospective workers needed to be prepared for hard outdoor work in a wild, untamed environment. Life in a lighthouse at the turn of the 20th century was hard. Norie read how keepers, their families and helpers, often isolated in remote locations, were at the mercy of weather and natural disasters. There were several forest fires that affected the areas surrounding lighthouses on Manitoulin Island. Burren Bay Lighthouse was mentioned in a few articles about a large fire occurring in the late 1800s. The fire, believed to have been caused by human carelessness, never reached the lighthouse but the smoke had greatly impacted the shipping lines resulting in hard, round the clock work for those tending the light and fog horn.

A couple of black and white poorly reproduced photos of Burren Bay lighthouse from the same period graced the pages of the magazine, and although the foliage around the structure wasn't present and the forest surrounding the cliff wasn't as thick as it was now, Norie recognized it immediately. She also recognized a reprint of the Easter Sunday 1910 photo she found in the storeroom. The images were less clear in the magazine reproduction, but there was an accompanying list of names of some of the people in the photo. Norie searched for anyone with the initials *O.M.* but found nothing.

The stories of lighthouse keepers' children who lived in the lighthouses from 1930 onward fascinated Norie. They were told by adults reminiscing about the good old days along the shores of the Great Lakes. As children they filled their days with home study, household and lighthouse chores and play. Many of the stories emphasized the freedom they had to explore along cliffs and beaches surrounding the Island lighthouses. While summer was wonderful, the shoulder seasons at the lighthouse were dangerous and uncomfortable.

"Mom is here."

Norie jumped when Wil spoke, and when she turned away, Norie swore she saw a little smirk on her face. She sighed, gathered the magazines scattered across the table and reshelved them. The isolation of lighthouse living was starting to sound pretty good to Norie.

On the return trip, after a late lunch at a quaint café, Wil chatted happily with her mother about their outing and the baking they would be doing on Thursday. Not once did she look at Norie. Not once did she acknowledge Norie's presence. Fine, Norie thought to herself. Let them talk on, mother and daughter, like the fools they were. She didn't need them anyway. Norie and her mother sat quietly, not even a glance shared between them all afternoon. Wil's words echoed in her head, "You called us!" A stray tear rolled down her cheek, and she quickly wiped it away. She had been watching the back of her mother's head since they left Prosper Bay. A new, wicked image from her nightmare flashed through her mind; her mother's empty, lifeless face staring at her from the steering wheel. Her mother dead. It wasn't the first time since the accident that the thought had crossed her mind. What if it were her mother who died in the accident? The insidious thought grew in her mind. It should have been Alice who was dead, not her father. She wouldn't be taking care of him right now. Nothing would have made him this way. He was too proud, too selfish. He would probably be involved in some new scheme, selling off something else someone loved. The thought satisfied her, but only for a moment before disgust and guilt upset her sense of satisfaction. Dahlia and Wil were giggling together over a joke Norie had missed. She brushed away another tear and turned to stare out the window.

It was early evening by the time they got back to Burren Bay. Norie didn't even go into the house. She headed toward the lighthouse, to the cliff, to the drawing rock. She felt safe enclosed in the tree branches, protected from the wind, and warmed by the heat the stone surface collected from the sun throughout the day. She sat quietly, too tired now to think, to ruminate. Her eyelids got heavy as she relaxed back onto the boulder beneath her.

She was almost asleep when she saw her—a girl in a long dress or maybe a nightgown walking across the alvar. She had long hair that was gathered into a loose ponytail below her neckline. The evening light made it difficult to see the colour of her hair or her clothes. She was a vision in sepia, like the amber of a charcoal sketch that had not yet been fixed to the page with resin. A chipmunk chittered in the trees closest to Norie and her attention was drawn away for a split second. When she looked back toward the girl, she was gone. Norie sat forward on the rock scanning the whole cliff. She got up and ran toward the lighthouse along the cliff's edge in case the girl had fallen over. There wasn't any evidence of that. She reached the lighthouse as the sun's sinking rays were hitting its walls. She ran around the whole structure and checked the door. She moved toward the foghorn building, circling the structure and checking the lock on the front door. It was secure too and the girl was nowhere to be seen. Norie was uncertain what to do next. Did she really see someone? She wasn't sure now. She had been almost asleep. Maybe she only imagined her. Maybe it was the girl she had seen in the village the first day they arrived. Perhaps she lived beyond the lighthouse, somewhere on the Rocky Plains First Nation. But the forest beyond the foghorn building was dense and black. How would anyone be able to find their way through it? Deciding that the girl had been part of some weird dream, Norie made her way back to the cottage. Her head was starting to ache with exhaustion. She just needed a good night's sleep.

# CHAPTER 12

*Burren Bay, July 1892*

Oonagh sat on the rock, the wooden board her father had made for her to use when sketching outdoors, lying firmly across her lap. The pouch she wore around her neck nestled where the board rested against her stomach. She looked out toward the bay, a bay she had come to call Little Burren Bay, as it bore only a passing resemblance to the sea waters flowing at the bottom of the cliffs, the edge of her Burren back home. Still, she had come to know this bay over the last months, sketching its character with the few pieces of charcoal that survived the journey across the ocean. The memory of the day she and Nan had made the charcoal over a wood fire in the yard was one she often conjured when she was feeling lonely. Tonight, though she missed Nan terribly, she felt peaceful and content. It was early evening, her favourite time to sketch, when the light rode the waves, bright and excited on the crests of each, only to disappear into darkness when the water rolled and crashed against itself. The fresh air, still warm from the day's heat, bathed her damaged lungs, and she felt robust and strong.

She had been told her mother was an artist like her, that her gift came through her maternal line from one woman to another. She supposed there were a few artistic men along the way, but hard-working Irish farmers had little time and opportunity to develop those skills and eventually the women took ownership of the talent in the family lore. Her proudest moment, sure to live on in family history, was when Da made a frame for a sketch she had done of the bay near their village. It had hung on the parlour wall of her grandparents' cottage back home. She was still surprised it made the voyage to the lighthouse without so much as a crack in the glass purchased from the landlord to protect the sketch in its wooden frame. Now she was determined to sketch this bay as well, this new Burren Bay that was to be her home at least until mid-November, when the living conditions would be impossible and the lighthouse unnecessary due to the winter freeze. Her fingers absentmindedly caressed the beaded pouch of stones as she took stock of the scene before her.

She settled further back on the rock and opened the tea tin where she stored her charcoal and sketching tools. With a piece of charcoal in hand, Oonagh began to lay the rough lines, both thick and thin, of the scene before her—the rocky edge along the cliff, the crevices that crisscrossed over the surface like the stitching of a crazy quilt, the soft fluid sweep of the tree line in the distance. She loved the way the soft blending of the charcoal across the paper made images ethereal and delicate, as if being viewed from behind a gauzy curtain. She used a feather to blend and smooth lines and shapes. With a leather stump Oonagh could erase charcoal lines and smudges, causing a play between light and dark on the page. She understood that the charcoal drawing was most effective when the artist picked and chose her details carefully. As she squinted at the scene before her, she instinctively knew which details she would include in the piece. It wasn't important that everything she saw be in the final drawing. This sketch was her interpretation. Her view of the landscape around her. It was as much about emotion as it was about reality.

She worked the charcoal until the light became too dim and the damp coolness of the evening caused her lungs to tighten and her shoulders to curl inward protectively around her chest. Oonagh wrapped her shawl around her shoulders and returned to the warmth of the lighthouse. Her father was in his bedroom completing the keeper's daily log. Her older brothers spent the night on duty, one at the foghorn station, the other at the top of the light tower keeping the light shining. Her youngest brother, two years older than her, was completing his reading for the day. Their father insisted they continue to study daily and managed to convince his contacts in the Department of Marine and Fisheries to secure materials for each of them to work through. While Oonagh enjoyed reading and doing her schoolwork, her first love was for her art. Sitting at the table with only the light of the oil lamp, she finished the sketch. She would affix the charcoal tomorrow with resin applied to the back of the paper. For now, she surveyed her work, proud of what she accomplished.

"So, have you finally finished?" Her brother had closed his books and stood by the table to see her work. "Beautiful as ever. Another masterpiece for framing I should think." Oonagh blushed. Although she basked in the praise, she couldn't help but be a little shy about it.

"Do you think so, Liam?"

"I do," said her brother. "In fact, I'm the one who will make the frame for it this time. Don't know where I'll find the glass, though. Maybe there are scraps in the old store shed."

"The frame alone would be lovely. Until then I'll keep it safe in my room." Her brother nodded and made his way to the room he shared with his brothers.

"Don't forget to sign it, though. It may be worth something one day."

Oonagh took the thinnest piece of charcoal from the tea tin and in the corner of the sketch carefully printed her initials, *O.M.*. Oonagh Murphy. Perhaps her work would one day hang in the great art galleries of the world. Perhaps she would be the one in the family to take her talent to a whole new level. She smiled at her own youthful hopefulness as she made her way up the stairs to her bedroom.

# CHAPTER 13

Norie awoke well before sunrise curled up on her bed, fully clothed from the night before, the pouch of stones still stuffed in her pocket. She had fallen asleep, exhausted and hot, but even that couldn't keep the nightmare from playing out in her subconscious. Only now, the girl from the lighthouse—the dream girl—was present, flitting in and out of the accident scene, taking her turn at the wheel. Wil lay asleep across from her and Norie was glad she hadn't awakened her. She couldn't bear the pity in Wil's eyes as she tried to sooth her, as she tried to understand.

She glanced down at the backpack sitting on the floor. She could see the tea tin sticking out of it, the corner of the lid still bearing the remnants of rust and age. She stared at it for a few seconds longer before leaning over and pulling it out. She removed the lid and instantly an odour of earth and pungent oils escaped the tin. She sat on the edge of the bed, breathing in the scent deeply, the tea tin balanced on her knees. The lid, which she laid on the edge of the bed beside her, slid to the floor noiselessly cradled by cast off blankets. She didn't notice, her eyes riveted on the thin strips of charcoal at the bottom of the tin. Movement in the air around her urged her to reach into the tin, coaxing her to pick up one of the pieces, to sketch. She contemplated the feel of the charcoal, soft and smooth in her hand. Finally, she reached into the tin and grasped one of the pieces, the weight of it light in her fingertips, its texture silky to the touch. She was surprised that it didn't leave black residue on her skin like the charcoal they used in drawing class. She glanced down to the backpack again, toying with the idea of trying the charcoal on a clean, creamy piece of paper in the sketchbook Dahlia had given her. The air around her moved a little faster, gathering along her bare arms, showing them the way to reach out for the sketchbook. Suddenly the moment was disturbed by voices, faint voices coming from the kitchen through a grate in the attic floor that had been uncovered when Gibson removed the boxes stored in the corner. Quickly she returned the charcoal to the can, replaced the tin's lid, and tucked it back into her backpack.

She got out of bed and tiptoed to the far corner of the room. Norie froze when one of the floorboards creaked, but the voices below continued to murmur, oblivious to her movement. She got down on the floor to listen, closer to the grate, closer to the conversation. The floor was surprisingly cool in the attic which was getting hotter as the summer progressed. A fan Gibson had moved up into the girls' bedroom sat in the corner ready to be plugged in and turned on when the heat got unbearable. They were two days away from opening the tearoom and museum. From what she was told, the tourist season was short in Burren Bay but brisk. She was expecting to hear Dahlia's voice itemizing everything that was still to be done, but instead she heard her mother's voice.

"She will never forgive me, Dahlia. I've screwed up too many times. I have no chances left." Norie could hear sniffling in between her words. "We've never really been close and this whole thing has driven an even bigger wedge between us." Anger began to settle in Norie's chest. Anger and trepidation. She should turn away now, she thought, but she couldn't.

"What do you mean, 'never been close'? She's your daughter! She loves you! She's taken care of you single handedly since the accident. By herself. Everything from appointments to medication. Alice, she loves you," Dahlia responded. Norie had taken care of her mother, but it was hard and almost as traumatic as the accident. That's why she called Dahlia in the first place. A teenager is not supposed to take care of a parent the way Norie had to. Norie knew Dahlia would be unable to understand how a mother and daughter could just grow apart. She and Wil were not like them. Her mother was right. They were not close. Wil shifted on her bed, rolling onto her side. Not like Dahlia and Wil. Alice worked all the time and took care of the house and waited on her father. She never had time for Norie.

"Talk to her. The two of you have been through a very traumatic event. You need to talk to her."

"I can't. I just can't." Or won't thought Norie.

"Alice, you can't let this happen all over again...I mean the depression and anxiety. The way Rory treated you last time you almost didn't make it." Last time. What last time, wondered Norie? She didn't know about a last time. "Norie needs to know. She's not a child anymore."

"No! I'm not ready. Not yet anyway."

"You will never be ready if you're waiting for the perfect moment. There are no perfect moments when you're trying to mend a relationship."

"You don't understand, Dahlia."

"Then help me understand. What could you have possibly done

that would ruin your relationship with Norie forever?" There was a long pause. Norie could hear the sliding of a chair as one of the women got up. She could hear the cupboard door and the running of the water. A million things ran through Norie's mind. Nothing could push them any further apart than they were right now.

"I didn't try to stop him. I knew." Lying flat on the floor, ear to the grate, Norie froze.

"Knew what?" Dahlia asked, exasperation in her voice.

"I knew Rory was trying to sell her art box. I knew where he was going that night. I'm the one who told him she had it in her backpack." Norie was stunned. She could feel the muscles in her arms and legs tighten and her skin turn cold. "She kept it hidden, but I told him. I wanted to taunt him with it. I knew he would try to take it and sell it. I wanted Norie to really see the kind of man he was and to stand up to him. But he got her in the car with it, and I didn't try hard enough to stop him or let her know."

Norie felt like throwing up. Her mother had done nothing to stop her father that night because she was the one who started it all. She betrayed Norie by telling her father that she had the art box all along. She hadn't uttered a word. When did she tell? How long had he known? Norie couldn't breathe. She needed to get outside. She didn't care how much noise she made now. She didn't care if she woke Wil. She didn't care if the women in the kitchen heard. She just didn't care. She clumsily stood and staggered to her bed. She grabbed her flip flops off the floor and ran down the stairs. The commotion she caused as she ran recklessly from the attic brought her mother and Dahlia running from the kitchen.

"Norie! Stop! Let me explain!"

"You've explained enough!" Norie yelled as the screen door slammed behind her. She ran down the lighthouse path and out onto the rock pavement. It wasn't yet light enough to see well and she stumbled in her flip flops. She made her way along the tree line to her spot amongst the cedars, to her hiding place on the rock. As she scrambled into the space, the tree branches folded in, hiding her from her mother and Dahlia. She could hear their voices calling, and saw them when they made the clearing as the sun began to rise. She watched them search for her for several minutes before Dahlia grabbed her mother by the arms. She spoke to her briefly and then pulled her mother into an embrace as her mother sobbed. They turned and made their way back to the tearoom.

Norie was numb. She had been betrayed by both of her parents—by her father's attempt to sell the art box and her mother's refusal to keep their secret. They had betrayed Norie and her grandmother. She pulled the pouch of stones from her pocket and emptied its contents into her hand. She squeezed her hand shut, the points of the stones piercing her skin. The pain made her feel alive when all she would rather do was just die. Why couldn't it have been her mother who died in the accident? Would it have mattered? Wouldn't it have just left her alone with her father and a lifetime of lies and betrayal? Her pain and anger turned to a wave of sadness, and she curled up and rocked her body back and forth on the hard stone until she dozed off hidden amongst the cedar trees.

*Her mother's lifeless body was slumped over the steering wheel, blood running freely from her ear and from a gash on her head. No this is wrong. This isn't the dream. This is not how it happened. She opened her mouth to scream but was choked by the smoke and the heat of the flames. She looked away from the fire and was distracted by movement beyond the car window. Looking out she saw her father standing only a few feet from the car, watching her.*

*"Help us," she screamed.*

*He didn't move at all. He stood staring at Norie as she screamed at him to get help. Then slowly, almost imperceptibly, he shook his head no.*

"Norie, are you alright?" Norie was roused by Wil's voice. "I know you're in there. Mom sent me to find you." She sounded annoyed and waited a minute or two before she spoke again. "Look, Nell will be here in a couple of hours, and you promised to help her hang her work." Norie sat up, pushing away the branches so she could see Wil.

"How did you know I was here?" Norie crawled off the rock. The mid-morning sun was blazing down on the rock pavement. Wil was clearly miffed.

"Are you kidding me? I've seen you sitting here before. I'm not stupid Norie. I'm aware of all kinds of things even if I don't act arrogant about it. Mom wants you back to help Nell." She waited until Norie stood before turning to walk away. Norie followed her back to the tearoom. Wil joined her mother in the kitchen. As Norie made her way down the hall to the bathroom she paused to watch her mother lying on her bed through the partially open bedroom door. Her eyes were closed, her cheeks and jaw were slack with sleep. She looked pale and small on the bed, but Norie couldn't help the rise of anger in her chest. The nightmare flashed through her mind, the new nightmare with her mother dead and her father refusing to help her. This was her new reality. This is what everything had come to. She stepped away from the doorway and into the bathroom to shower away the heaviness of the morning heat. As she dressed later, she realized the shorts she was wearing had no pockets, no place to hold the pouch of rocks she had grown accustomed to carrying with her. Instead, she slipped the leather thong around her neck. Tucking the pouch under her t-shirt, she headed downstairs.

Nell arrived after lunch and Norie helped her unload and carry several paintings and the necessary tools for hanging them in the cottage. Norie watched as she wandered around the tearoom, measuring blank spaces on the walls, rearranging the artwork that was already there, and leaning her work against the wall where she intended to hang things. As Nell disappeared into the hall, Norie perused the paintings the artist had chosen for the show. They were all lighthouses on Manitoulin Island. All framed in rustic wood frames and double matted in taupe and charcoal grey. She recognized the Burren Bay lighthouse and could even tell where Nell sat when she did her preliminary sketches.

"This little drawing is lovely," Nell said, interrupting Norie's thoughts. She rounded the corner from the hallway with the framed charcoal sketch Norie too had noticed. "The charcoal work is primitive, but the effect is quite charming." She held the sketch up to the light. "*O.M.*? Any idea who that is?"

"No, but I found two more of their sketches in the lighthouse when we were cleaning out a storage room." Nell brought the sketch over to Norie for them both to examine together in better light.

"I think it's old. You see these wispy strokes here, along the cliff edge?" Norie moved in closer to examine the picture. "That was probably done with a feather. Nowadays we have all kinds of brushes and fancy tools to create this effect with charcoal. But back in the day people used what was in the natural environment. In fact, can you see how the charcoal has a brown tint to it? Probably homemade charcoal."

"The other two sketches have the same tint to them."

"If a stick of charcoal hasn't completely burned and still has some green on one end, the burnt end looks brown, like this. Could I see the other sketches?" Nell asked.

"I'll get them." Norie ran up to the attic and retrieved the smaller sketches from her backpack.

"These are lovely too," Nell said as she examined them. "Oh, I see. These are Burren Bay here from the cliff. I wonder where this bay is?" She pointed to the framed picture.

"I think it's a place in Ireland. Burren Bay was named after an area called The Burren in Ireland." Norie said.

"That makes sense. Many of the bays on the Island are named after some other place or sometimes people." Nell paused for a moment then asked, "Have you worked with charcoal?"

"A little. In my art class," Norie replied.

"If you like," returned Nell, "We could try our hand at making charcoal together. I haven't done it since art school, like a million years ago. Let's try." Norie didn't know what to say. "I'll get in touch after opening day. I can't imagine Dahlia letting me take you for a few hours until the tourist rush settles a bit." Norie breathed again not realizing that she was holding her breath. She had time to think up an excuse. Time to come up with why she couldn't possibly do something related to art—the one thing she loved that started the whole mess in the first place. Nell interrupted her thoughts, "Now let's get hanging!"

The remainder of the afternoon was spent hanging the lighthouse paintings and mounting description and price cards on the wall beside the pictures. After Nell left, Norie returned the sketches to the attic, tucking them into the empty sketchbook in her backpack for safe keeping. She pulled out the tea tin and stared at it for a long time, hearing each tick of the bedside clock as she stood there. She could easily pull the lid off, pick up a piece of charcoal and start sketching on the clean, empty pages of the sketchbook. The heat and humidity in the room hung heavy around her shoulders. It was just a can full of charcoal and feathers. Some other artist's tools of the trade. After everything that had taken place, knowing everything that she knew, how could she even contemplate using them. She returned the tin to her bag and left the attic.

# CHAPTER 14

The day before opening day—the soft launch Dahlia had called it—began bright and warm. They all found themselves in the kitchen waiting for Dahlia to start the circle of belonging. Gibson had left again on another long haul. His frequent absences reminded Norie of her father. At least he was usually at home. Although when her father was at home, he wasn't present anyway. When it came time to hold hands, Norie took Wil's hand without hesitation. Wil took her hand without so much as a glance her way.

"Circle us, keep hope within, and despair without," Dahlia began. "Circle us, keep peace within, and worry without." Norie glanced at her mother. Her head was lowered as if in deep prayer. Her long, thin hair hung limply around her face and appeared unwashed and uncombed. For all her faults, slovenliness was not a part of her mother's character. Every uniform of every job her mother had was impeccably kept. Norie rarely saw her mother wear make-up, but her hair was always tidy and clean. The image of her mother asleep after their argument yesterday flashed through her mind. Good. At least she wasn't the only one unhappy right now. It served her mother right. She lied, a lie of omission. She told secrets shared in confidence. She let Norie think that only her father had betrayed her the night of the accident. It was easy to pin it on him. He was always scheming and hustling. He was dead.

"Circle us, keep love within, and hatred without."

Her heart ached for the lost art box. For Grandma Johanna. Maybe it even ached a little for her father. She had memories, images really, of Rory playing with her when she was little. Images of him sitting on the floor of her closet playing with her and her doll house. She had glimpses of him in her mind reading to her at bedtime. Building a snowman. Making sandcastles at the beach. She wasn't sure when it all changed. Yes, her heart ached a little for her father, but right now, her heart was stone where her mother was concerned.

"Circle us, keep courage within, and fear without. Circle us, keep light within, and darkness without." Dahlia finished the prayer and they all released their hands. "So today is the soft launch of the tearoom and museum. I've invited fifteen or twenty people from the village and a few other friends from around the Island to come here for a couple of hours this afternoon, so we can perfect our systems and identify things we're missing or things we need to change." Wil circled the table pouring tea and handing out tea biscuits. "You two girls will work the desk and give informal tours out at the lighthouse and Alice you and I will take care of the tearoom. We aren't collecting money today. It's all free for our friends. The baking is done so it's just a matter of making tea and coffee and preparing light lunch orders. I also made a batch of iced tea. It doesn't feel like this heat is letting up anytime soon." Norie glanced out the window to watch the birds feed on the windowsill crumbs. Every morning someone, Dahlia she guessed, freshened the crumbs and every morning the birds fed on them.

"Dahlia," Alice's voice interrupted the birds' breakfast. "Would you and Wil give Norie and I a moment alone please? Just a few minutes." The silence in the kitchen was deafening. Norie had heard that saying before but never really understood what it meant until now. Wil froze and looked to her mother for direction. Norie's stomach flip-flopped, and she was unable to move, to escape. She placed her hand over the pouch of stones hidden under her t-shirt to steady herself. Dahlia studied Alice's face for a few seconds before nodding her head and grabbing Wil's hand to haul her from the kitchen.

"I just want to apologize to you for yesterday...for everything. I didn't want you to find out that way, but I couldn't find the right time or the right way to explain." Alice took a deep breath. Norie found her voice.

"You don't have to explain. I understand everything. You told him I had the box. You knew what Dad was going to do, and you didn't stop him." She tried to keep her voice even, and tried not to cry. "You knew how much Grandma Johanna's box meant to me. She was your mother!"

"I know that, but your father could be...ruthless. There's a lot you don't know about. A lot of things that happen between adults...that's not the point right now. I want to apologize for not keeping the secret and then not saying something to let you know or to stop your father. I apologize for not saying something." Her mother paused for a moment and Norie waited, holding her breath. Alice continued, "That's all. You don't have to accept it. I just...that's all. I'm sorry." Alice stopped abruptly and got up and left the room. Norie sat stunned for a few moments. She didn't know if she was more surprised by the apology or the abruptness of it. The tears that threatened to fall were replaced by anger and disappointment. It was not the apology she wanted or expected. Alice was sorry but not for the years of being emotionally absent from her daughter. Not sorry for letting Norie learn her father's true nature, his selfishness and arrogance on her own. Not sorry for helping Norie to see why her father was the way he was. Not sorry for forcing Norie into the caregiver role after the accident. She stayed sitting in the kitchen for a few minutes more listening to her mother gathering things in her bedroom, going into the washroom, and closing the door.

Wil and Norie had a full two hours of lighthouse tours. Some of the guests from the village who had lived in Burren Bay their whole lives knew more about the lighthouse than either of them. Mrs. Kingstown, who lived in a century home on a hill overlooking the village, had grown up, married and raised her family in Burren Bay. Norie was guiding her through the tour when the old woman stopped and gazed at the lighthouse dining room table.

"My father and Mr. Peterson, I think he was the lighthouse keeper in around 1940, were good friends. We often came out here for picnics on Sunday afternoons after church. It was great fun!" For a moment, her eyes glazed over as she lost herself in the memories of the past. "This table would have been piled high with food. Both Mrs. Peterson and my mother were excellent cooks! I loved baking with my mother. Do you and your mother bake or cook together?" The question caught Norie off guard. Her mother and her did nothing together.

"Not really," she recovered, "My mom had more than one job back home, so there wasn't really time."

"Oh, that's too bad, dear. Modern life has taken such a bite out of the pleasures we had as young people." Norie nodded in agreement. She really couldn't remember a time when she and her mother hung out together. When Norie was a girl, she recalled playground visits and maybe playdates with neighbours, but once she started school and her father lost his job, Norie only had memories of her mother rushing out the door to work.

"Oh my, I haven't seen one of these since I was a girl!" Mrs. Kingstown was enthralled with the various antiques on display on the old sideboard. She took an item in her shrunken, shaky hands. It was a small metal tin shaped like a teapot. It looked like the small metal teapots that restaurants served tea in, the ones that were impossible to pour without tea leaking all over the place. Only this teapot was old and roughly made. There was surface rust on the edges of the tin, but the original metal didn't seem to be damaged at all.

"Isn't it a teapot?" asked Norie.

"Oh no, not a teapot." Mrs. Kingstown turned the item over in her hands, holding it firmly against her as she pried the top off. A small bundle fell out onto the floor, rolling under the sideboard. Norie squatted and retrieved it. Mrs. Kingstown placed the empty tin on the sideboard, her face lighting up as Norie placed the bundle in her now empty hands. The old woman unwrapped the small package revealing two pale yellow beeswax candles, about two inches long.

"It's a candle tin. Candles, wicks, and matches would be stored in here," she pointed to the base of the tin, "And then a candle would sit on the top in this little well." She picked up one of the candle stubs and set it in the lid of the tin.

"How old do you think this is?" asked Norie.

"Well, I'm not an antiques expert, but I am old enough to remember using them to go to the outhouse in the middle of the night! I imagine they were common before electricity became widely available. I don't know..." her voice trailed off and her eyes glazed over again in memory. Only this time, her memory seemed to be disturbing to her.

"Are you okay, Mrs. Kingstown?" Norie supported her arm as she moved to sit down on an old bench nearby.

"Oh dear, just a memory I haven't had in a long time." She looked at Norie carefully, and Norie felt as if she were being sized up by a teacher preparing to hand out an important job. "Have..." the old woman's voice quivered, "Have you ever seen a ghost?"

"A ghost?" Norie's unease was growing.

"I don't mean the Halloween sort of white sheet nonsense. More of a presence or a spirit or a vision?" Norie instantly thought of the girl she had seen around the lighthouse. The thought of her being a ghost had crossed her mind, but she was 15 years old! She didn't believe in ghosts anymore. Mrs. Kingstown's eyes focused on Norie's as she began to recount her memory.

"The summer when Sarah Peters and I were both 12, we decided to have a sleepover at the lighthouse. In the middle of the night Sarah needed to use the outhouse, so she woke me up for company. We were silly girls back then, afraid of our own shadows for goodness sake." She looked over at the candle tin sitting on the sideboard. "Sarah's family had a few candle tins, not like that one," she pointed to the cabinet, "But, others that they used to walk to the outhouse at night."

"Anyway, we got up and lit the candle and headed to the privy. Sarah went inside to do her business, while I stood outside and waited. I know I was young and had a very overactive imagination, but while I was standing there, I saw a girl. She was a little older than I was, probably more your age," she glanced at Norie, then continued, "She moved around the lighthouse and along the cliff edge through the darkness. At first, I thought she was from the village, so I took a few steps toward her and called out, but then she just sort of vanished." Mrs. Kingstown looked back at Norie. "I haven't thought much of her in many, many years. That candle tin just stirred it up again. It just felt so real." She collected herself.

"Just ramblings from an old lady. I hope I didn't frighten you?"

"Oh no, don't worry about it. I don't frighten easily," replied Norie, but she could feel goosebumps on her arms even though it was a thousand degrees in the lighthouse. She touched the pouch of stones around her neck as if it were an amulet she wore for protection.

"Well, I think I've had enough of the tour for now, dear. Perhaps you wouldn't mind helping me make my way to the tearoom. I'm feeling a little peckish."

The soft launch for the tearoom went well, although they ran out of iced tea rather quickly. In the unusual heat of the early summer, guests were not interested in hot beverages. Dahlia and Alice spent the evening brewing pots of tea to make more of the iced variety while the girls had time to themselves. Norie walked out to the lighthouse to sit on her spot on the rock. She hadn't had time all day to think about her mother's apology earlier. Her anger had eased a little, but she still felt disappointed and sad. She had a whole summer ahead of her here surrounded by other people, Wil, Dahlia and Gibson. What would happen in the fall when she and her mother returned to their old lives?

"I thought I'd find you here," said Wil, interrupting her thoughts.

"I didn't see you coming," Norie said.

"That's because you're tucked into your sacred space."

"My what?"

"Your sacred space." Wil paused before she went on. She put down the foil covered plate she had been carrying. "My mom says the Celts believed that each of us is drawn to a special place of spiritual significance and that we return to that place over and over again to meditate or think or just to feel comfort. You come here a lot and so this must be a place like that for you." Norie surveyed the landscape around her as the sun began to sink slowly toward the horizon. It was rocky and wild, the sound of waves crashing just below the cliff's edge—a place where the wind sometimes picked up without warning, causing the trees to push out their branches and flail as if in ancient ritualistic celebration. Norie understood. She returned her gaze to Wil.

"Do you have a sacred space?"

"Well," Wil bit down on her lip, "I do, or did, back at our old place. There's a creek that flows out of one of the mine sites. It came down through the rocks behind our apartment building and flowed into the river that cuts through the city. There's a rock ledge that I loved to sit on. I could see all the way down the hillside to the backyard of my old elementary school. I think it was my sacred place." She paused and glanced out along the rock pavement. "I don't have any place here. Not yet anyway..." For the first time since coming to Burren Bay it struck Norie just how isolated it must have been for Wil to leave her home in the city and come here.

"What's on the plate?" asked Norie, trying to ignore the discomfort of intimacy the two were sharing.

"Oh, that's my idea," she was instantly animated, "My mom does this ritual every morning where she crumbles homemade fennel biscuits around the outside of the tearoom. I know it's not morning, but evening is every bit as powerful as morning." Wil lifted off the foil exposing two biscuits from the kitchen. "She breaks up the biscuits and sprinkles the crumbs along the stone foundation of the whole building and on the windowsills."

"Those are the crumbs I see the birds eating on the kitchen windowsill every morning! I was wondering about those."

"They're supposed to protect and purify our home. Mom says that fennel was believed to be a cleansing and protective plant. I don't know if I believe that completely, but after everything you've been through," Wil's voice quivered, "I thought you could use as much cleansing and protection as possible."

"Thanks. I'm sorry about the other day. Well, I guess I'm sorry about a few days..." Norie didn't know what else to say.

"That's okay. You really have had a crappy spring, and I guess I can cut you some slack."

She was touched, and Wil was right.

"So, how does this work?"

Wil took one of the tea biscuits, broke it in half, and handed one half to Norie. "This one we eat. I'm starved." The two girls devoured the biscuit. Norie realized with all the commotion that day, she hadn't eaten much since breakfast, and she was sure Wil hadn't either.

"Now we take this other biscuit," she paused to break it in half like the last one, "and crumble it around your rock. I'll go clockwise and you go counterclockwise." They circled the rock, sprinkling bits of biscuit as they went. They struggled with the back side of the alcove, fighting against the overhanging branches. They helped each other to step up onto the rock to sprinkle crumbs back into the trees and then met at the opening when they were done.

"There," stated Wil. "Now you are good to go. I promise to keep your sacred space a secret. Our mothers don't have to know everything." Norie knew about secrets, her mother and father had plenty, and they weren't particularly good at keeping them. "I really am starving now. Do you want to go have dinner? I'm sure there are leftovers from today."

Norie agreed, and the two girls walked together toward the trees and the tearoom. As they entered the path through the cedars, Norie glanced back toward her sacred space. As the sun set, the light across the rock pavement had begun to change, throwing shadows where shadows had not been only minutes before. She thought she saw movement near her rock, as if something or someone was sitting on the rock's outer edge, settling themselves into comfort. The story Mrs. Kingstown had told her that afternoon resurfaced in her mind. She kept walking as she stared over her shoulder trying to see in the dimming light. She was so focused on what was behind her, that she didn't watch where she was going and tripped on a tree root. When she looked back, she could see nothing. The sunset had thrown the area into darkness. Feeling a little uneasy, Norie rushed forward to catch up with Wil.

# CHAPTER 15

*Burren Bay, June 1892*

L iam had been gone for hours. Even Da was beginning to show signs of worry. Oonagh watched him from the kitchen window pacing along at the edge of the cliff and peering off into the thick bush surrounding the lighthouse. Her brother went off hunting for rabbit, but he should have been back by now. Her father's last-minute instructions to Liam were clear.

"Stay on lighthouse property Liam. We have no business on Indian land." The Indian Agent for the region had made it very clear to them when they arrived that they were to stay on lighthouse property only. Burren Bay Lighthouse butted up against Rocky Plain Indian Reserve. The Murphy's had no experience with the Canadian Indians other than those they saw at various ports and businesses on their way to Burren Bay. They had been warned by many locals to keep their distance. What Oonagh knew about the

Indians in Canada was what she had read in books and newspapers and it both angered and impressed her. She had long heard stories of the horrible treatment of her own people, especially during the Great Famine. It seems to her that the mistreatment of the Irish by the British was not all that different from what the Dominion of Canada was now doing to the Indians.

Oonagh had spent a good part of the day making Nan's *stobhach gaelach* for their evening meal. Nan said the best stew was her stew after the flavours of the ingredients had a chance to blend. The root vegetables, potatoes, and carrots, softening in the stock of the meat with Nan's seasonings and herbs, sat warming on the back of the stove. As she waited for Liam to return, she also prepared a loaf of soda bread. Flour, salt, baking soda and a little milk soured by vinegar when butter milk was a scarce commodity. The kneading of the dough relaxed her and at least for a few moments took away her growing worry. She placed the roughly formed loaf to cool on the kitchen windowsill. Putting her hand to her chest she could feel Nan's pouch under her bodice where she had tucked it while making the bread. Now, as she pulled it out and laid it against the placket of her dress, the small pouch felt warm and familiar.

A sudden cry from her older brother Patrick brought Oonagh to the door of the lighthouse. She could see her father and brothers looking westward into the forest, and she stepped out of the doorway to get a better look. Emerging from the forest was Liam, bent over and limping. He was supported on either side by two Indian boys about the same age as him. As they moved further into the clearing another Indian, an adult male, followed them. Next to this man was a younger boy. Oonagh guessed he was about 10 years old. She noticed their dress resembled her own family's clothing but adorned with beads and feathers. They wore deer hide shoes not unlike her own pampooties, moccasins she thought they were called, and had various straps and bags slung over their shoulders and attached to the belts around their waists. They stood on the edge of the property, wary and silent. Da moved forward first, motioning his sons to stay back. Oonagh moved closer into the clearing. Suddenly Liam spoke.

"Da. It's okay. They helped me back. They're just helping." Oonagh watched as her father made eye contact with the older man, nodding an assurance that everyone was calm, and no one was in danger. The two teens moved to help Liam over to a bench that sat on a rock terrace between the lighthouse and the foghorn building. Oonagh rushed over to him, kneeling on the ground in front of him, scanning for injuries. "I'm fine," he said. "I accidently stepped into one of those God forsaken cracks in the rock and twisted my ankle. I fell over and hit my head." Oonagh saw a small trickle of dried blood on his temple and a quick glance at his ankle showed swelling and bruising. The older Indian man spoke. Oonagh's family did not understand the words and his even, careful voice made it difficult to interpret his thoughts.

"*Nimishoomis* say we come to give back boy who hurt on our land." The youngest of their party had a reasonable grasp of English and was able to act as translator. "He no go *Asiniikmigaag Mashkodeng*." When he saw their confusion, he continued. "No go Rocky Plain. Many dangers there." Oonagh's father looked at the older man and nodded.

"Tell him we understand and are very sorry for causing a problem."

The young boy spoke rapidly to his companions. Oonagh recognized the cadence of Ojibwe that he spoke. The older man nodded back.

"Oonagh, go to the house and bring out the soda bread you baked this afternoon. We are going to share a bit of afternoon tea with our new neighbours."

She did what her father told her, carefully slicing the fresh loaf of bread, and placing slices in a basket with a small bowl of hand churned butter and a knife for spreading. She hurried back out to where her father stood. He turned to the young translator saying, "Tell *Nimishoomis* that we offer some of our food as an apology and a sign of our friendship." The young boy translated, and the older man nodded. Oonagh passed out the thick slices of bread, each one slathered with butter. The older man raised the piece to his nose then to his mouth biting into the bread first before the boys did. A smile instantly formed on his face, and he spoke rapidly to the young boy.

"*Nimishoomis* say your bannock good."

Relieved that Liam was back and that there were no hard feelings between them and their Indian neighbours, Oonagh breathed a sigh of relief. Her hand immediately grasped at the pouch that lay against her chest. She noticed the young boy looking at her. Excitedly he drew her attention to a small pouch that was fastened with a leather string to the belt around his waist. It was roughly the same size as her pouch but beautifully decorated with colourful beads in a stunning, intricate pattern. The pouch was fringed at the bottom with thin strips of deer hide. He untied the strap and motioned that he wanted to trade his pouch for hers. He nodded his head encouragingly and said, "*Gwii-meshkwadoonamaw na*? Trade?"

"Oh, I couldn't take it. It is so beautiful!"

"Nookomis make *gashkibidaagan*. She happy friend trade." Oonagh looked at her father and then to Mishomis. Both smiled encouragingly. She removed the pouch from around her neck, loosened the tie and removed the contents. The boy did the same thing and then they exchanged pouches replacing their own belongings in their newly acquired bag. As she placed the new pouch around her neck, she thought to herself how much like jewellery it was. Nan would equally be happy with this trade.

When the last piece of Oongah's bread was eaten Patrick moved to help Liam into the lighthouse to be attended to and to rest. The Indian party turned to leave the lighthouse and return to their home. They had almost disappeared into the tree line when the young boy turned and called out, "*Giga-waabamin!*" Then he disappeared into the bush. Oonagh laid her hand on her chest and felt the texture of the beaded pouch against her palm and smiled.

# CHAPTER 16

Norie watched as Gibson exited the path from the tearoom and headed toward the lighthouse. He walked with purpose, his long legs covering the ground between them quickly. Over the few weeks she had been in Burren Bay she had made no effort to get to know him or even like him. She would never have come to Dahlia's if she knew he was here. Every word of encouragement he gave her and every attempt to engage her in conversation made her distrustful of his intentions. He wasn't her father. He wasn't even Wil's father. He had no business being fatherly at all, and she felt that his kindness was all an act. She knew his attempts to interact with her were to please Dahlia and had nothing to do with genuine feelings. He had ulterior motives, she was certain. Just like her father.

The screen door banged as he pulled it open. When Gibson saw her sitting behind the counter, he smiled.

"Good morning Norie," he said, "How's it going?"

"Fine." She replied in as few words as possible pretending to be interested in the pamphlet laid out before her on the counter.

"Is Wil here?" His voice was light and sweet. "Dahlia said she was supposed to be working this morning. At least for a few hours. I've got to take her to Prosper Bay for a dental appointment."

"She's probably in the back or upstairs. I'm not her boss."

"I wasn't implying you were." Gibson said. "I just assumed you would have seen her. It's not like this is a big building." He moved through the entrance into the lighthouse and called for Wil. Norie could hear her answer back, but her exact words were muffled. Gibson moved back into the foyer to wait for her.

"She said she would be right down," he told Norie and then stood in awkward silence while he waited. "It's going to be hot again today," he said in another attempt to start a conversation, but Norie didn't look up from what she was reading. She refused to engage in any conversation with him. He knew nothing about her or what she had been through. He had nothing to offer her. "Ray Fox will be in tomorrow, finally, to do the repairs. He's so busy he couldn't get here before our opening." Norie continued to read.

"Why don't you come with Wil and I into town for her appointment today? You can both have some time to look around a few shops. Maybe go to the library."

"If I'm not here, who will work the front desk? Maybe you better check with Dahlia before you start making plans." Her father had tried to control everything too. That was never going to happen again.

"Look, I know we don't know each other very well, but we could try to be friendly with each other."

"I don't want to be friendly with you. You are not my friend. You are not even my mother's friend. You just happen to be married to Dahlia. You aren't even Wil's father so stop trying to father me."

"I'm not trying to father you Norie. I can't possibly replace your dad. Being a dad is so much more—" Wil entered the foyer as Norie lashed out.

"What do you know about being a father?" Norie spit out, only half hearing the gasp from Wil. "You are hardly here most of the time and when you are you act like you're the boss of everything." Wil moved further into the foyer.

"You know what, I'm pretty much done with your self-centred, egocentric bull right now." Gibson moved toward the counter closer to Norie. She stared at him defiantly.

"Gib, let's just go," Wil said in a quiet voice.

"No Wil. It's time someone sets her straight about life, death and grief."

"And what do you know about grief?" Norie yelled.

"Oh, I don't know. Maybe the next time I go to the cemetery to visit the grave of my dead wife and baby boy, you can come and give me some pointers." Gibson's voice shook with a mixture of grief and anger. Norie's chest tightened, and she shrank back in her chair as he spoke.

"They both died in a horrible car accident, just like the one you were in. And you know the worse part? I don't know if it really was an accident. And every week I visit them and beg my dead wife for a sign that it was all just a mistake. Bad weather. Road conditions." Wil moved forward and touched Gibson's arm. He looked at her and then back to Norie.

"Wil, I'll meet you at the house." Then he turned and hurried out of the lighthouse.

Norie sat, stunned into silence. She didn't know what to say. She couldn't say anything that would have excused her horrible behaviour. She looked at Wil, her voice strained with emotion. "I didn't know."

"You couldn't have known," Wil paused for a moment. "That's why you can't judge anyone before you really get to know them.

That's why you have to give people a chance." Wil glanced out the door at the figure of Gibson hurrying across rock pavement. "Gib is a good guy, Norie. I don't know everything that happened in your family, but I know it wasn't good. Don't judge other people by your experience. Gibson hasn't tried to replace my father, and he isn't trying to do that to you. He just knows what you're going through, probably more than any of us, and wants to help. He's just being supportive. He's worried about you and your mom." She paused again. "I gotta go...I'll see you when I get back."

"I'm so sorry," Norie said, her voice small with regret and embarrassment.

"I know you are. But sometimes that's not enough." Wil left Norie sitting at the desk. For the first time since the accident Norie was thinking about someone other than herself.

# CHAPTER 17

The museum had been closed for three days while repairs were made to the roof and the damage the leaks caused inside the building. The two girls were kept busy with jobs around the tearoom. They spent almost a whole day dusting Dahlia's teapot collection in the *Jolly Pot Teapot Museum* housed in a room off the main serving area. Norie had never seen so many teapots in one place, and if she was being honest with herself, she enjoyed seeing what was there. They counted 117 teapots, no doubles and a few so old their surfaces were faded and honeycombed. Now as she lugged a soft-sided cooler under the intense noon sun out to the lighthouse—lunch for the contractor, Ray Fox—Norie wished she was back in the teapot museum sitting and dusting in the cool breeze of the fan.

Norie also wished she could go back in time to change the horrible things she said to Gibson. She had no idea he'd been married before and clueless of the tragedy he experienced. She was embarrassed by her self-centredness and coldness. He lost his wife and baby all at once. Like her, he knew the weight of pain and grief. In her mind she could hear her grandmother's scolding. Grandma Johanna would never have behaved so poorly and so cruelly. Is this what she was becoming?

As she stumbled over the hidden roots of trees along the path, the cooler shifted on her shoulder catching the pouch of stones around her neck. Worried that the rubbing of the cooler against her body would damage the old beaded pouch, Norie placed the cooler on the ground and removed it from around her neck. She wrapped the leather thong around a belt loop on the side of her shorts securing it against her hip. Norie's fingers lingered on the soft, weathered fabric, sliding across the smoothness of its shiny surface. An image flashed in her mind of her Grandma Johanna's fingers sliding across the lid of the old artist's box. The memory brought a strange mixture of peace and pain. Norie sighed, picked up the cooler and continued on to the lighthouse.

She found Ray in the small storage room under the stairs. He was finishing the final layer of plaster on the walls, smoothing out the surfaces with a trowel and rags. He was a big man, not very tall, but stout and muscular. He wore a plaid work shirt, jeans, and work boots. His long black hair was pulled into two braids down his back and his brown skin glistened with sweat.

"Hey, Norie," he said, backing out of the room.

"Hey. Dahlia sent out a picnic lunch for you again. It's on the table. When you're done just pile everything back into the cooler like yesterday, and someone will come back and get it." Ray looked over Norie's shoulder and nodded.

"*Miigwetch*. Listen Norie, can you give me a hand before you leave? I tacked the drop cloth in the corner but the lighting in here is terrible and I can't find the little nail I used. Freakin' old eyes, eh? Can you hold the work lamp for me for a second?"

"Sure." With the work lamp in hand, Norie squeezed into the back corner of the storage room, careful not to rub up against the wet plaster. Ray crouched in the corner.

"There you are. You little bugger." As he reached up to adjust the lamp in Norie's hand, he noticed the beaded bag tied to her belt loop. "Hey! That's a cool little tobacco pouch you have. I didn't know you chewed tobacco."

"Ha! Very funny," Norie said, acknowledging his teasing. Ray pulled the nail and the two backed out of the little storage room pulling the drop cloth as they went.

"I found it out here by the lighthouse." She untied the pouch and handed it to Ray to examine.

"Long ago my people used a lot of these little pouches, kind of like pockets. And they carried more than tobacco in them." He laughed. "I have one my *Nookomis* made for me."

"*Nookomis*?" Norie asked. The word sounded familiar. It was a word she might have learned during the Indigenous cultural programs she attended in elementary school. She liked the sound of the word, the way the syllables, the vowels and consonants, bumped against each other when Ray spoke.

"My grandmother." Grandmother. Of course. Now she remembered. "She was an amazing craftswoman and we spent a lot of time together when I was a kid. My parents worked, you know, so she took care of me." Ray drew Norie's attention to the small, beaded pouch tied to his belt. "It's old but not as old as yours. I usually carry tobacco in it, but sometimes I put matches, screws, nails, sometimes money. You name it, I've carried it in my *gashkibidaagan*." Norie could see the intricate bead work on the pouch forming a stylized picture of an animal. "But now I got pockets! They're helpful too," he laughed.

"Is that a bear?" She looked intently at the fine bead work and patterns.

"Yup. That's my clan. *Doodem*. We are warriors and medicine gatherers traditionally." Ray examined the pouch Norie found. "I can't really tell what the design was on this pouch. Most of the beads have fallen off." He handed it back to Norie. "What do you keep in it?"

"Stones." Norie loosened the neck of the bag and showed Ray the three small stones that she found. "I'm pretty sure they come from the rocks around the lighthouse."

"Could be. Maybe not though." He examined the stones carefully before returning them to the pouch. "You take care of this Norie. You probably didn't find it. It found you. Now you gotta be its keeper." He moved toward the table and the cooler. "Now for lunch! I wonder what yummies Dahlia gave me today." Norie watched as Ray emptied the cooler, examining the contents of each container and baggie. His palms were broad and thick with the strength of a contractor, but his fingers were long and nimble, opening and closing the lunch items with the dexterity of a craftsman. An artist. Like his grandmother. Like his *Nokomis*. Like her Grandma Johanna. Norie took a deep breath, emboldened by her grandmother's memory. "Can I ask you a question, Ray?" He looked up at her and nodded, his mouth too full of Dahlia's delicious egg salad to speak. "You've been friends with Gibson for a long time. Right?" Ray finished chewing and took a long drink from a water bottle before answering.

"Gib and I went to elementary school together in Prosper Bay. We've been friends ever since. He's a good guy."

"What happened with his wife? I mean his first wife."

"Well," Ray seemed to choose his words carefully. "It was late spring, and Jules and the baby were coming back to the Island from a doctor's appointment on the mainland. The conditions were lousy and as far as I know, she lost control and swerved into an oncoming truck. Police report said she and the little guy were killed instantly." It was an accidental situation Norie was all too familiar with and she felt her lungs constrict and her muscles tense. It also seemed to Norie that he had given her the polite version of the story.

"What sort of woman was she?"

"Jules? I don't know...she was nice enough. I liked her." Norie looked at Ray and he added, "She was troubled, I think. Always struggling. After the baby was born, she had a hard time coping." Norie nodded, her embarrassment about how she had treated Gibson foremost in her mind. "What's with all the questions about Jules and the accident?"

"I don't know. Just trying to understand the situation. Trying to figure my own things out."

Ray smiled and nodded. "I know you and your mom have been through a lot. You need to be patient with yourself and your mom. Now, you want to share this piece of pie with me?" Norie laughed.

"No. I got chores at the tearoom to do before my lunchtime. I'll see you later Ray."

"Okay. *Giga-waabamin*. Take it easy."

As Norie made her way back to the tearoom, her anger and disappointment with herself for how she had judged Gibson was palpable. How was she ever going to get through this whole mess? She had made so many mistakes. Even the coolness of the path back to the tearoom couldn't lift the hot heaviness she felt.

# CHAPTER 18

*Burren Bay, May 1892*

Oonagh shivered and coughed as she stepped through the doorway. It was colder inside than out, the dampness of the winter still captured within the plaster and lathe of the lighthouse walls. It sat exposed to the elements, waiting to be released by the promise of spring. A loud bang startled her, and light suddenly filled the kitchen. Liam put his cherub face against the glass and pulled a funny expression.

"Hey Oonagh!" he yelled, getting her attention. The windows had been boarded up since last November when the shipping lanes began freezing over and the old keeper and his family moved out. Now they were slowly being freed as her youngest brother unbolted and laid the shutters back against the whitewashed clapboard.

"Don't be so foolish," she scolded, but secretly she loved Liam's foolish ways.

Her father and two older brothers were off somewhere tending to the other hundreds of tasks on the list the man from the Department of Marine and Fisheries had given them. Much was to be done to get the lighthouse and foghorn station up and running before the end of the month. Here, in Burren Bay, was where the waters of Lake Huron met the waters of the North Channel. It was a prime shipping route between Canada and the United States of America. The mouth of the bay was treacherous and the Burren Bay lighthouse and foghorn necessary for safe travel.

The house seated around the lighthouse tower was to be Oonagh's domain. The interior anyway. She made her way through the kitchen noting the woodstove, cupboards, and shelving. A few chipped dishes and empty tins had been left behind. A pile of wood sat on the floor beside the woodstove, and she made a mental note to ask her father to check the chimney for debris, fallen stones or bird nests, before she started a fire to warm the house. She stopped on the threshold between the kitchen and dining room, overcome by wheezing and coughing. Her young body was wracked by fatigue and illness brought on by a difficult ocean crossing and several weeks in quarantine. She gazed around the barren room, acutely aware of the fact that she was the only woman of the house now. Back home it was the women in a house that made it a home. The women who worked together to gather and cook food, mend clothing, and keep the hearth light burning. Mothers, daughters, daughters-in-law, grandmothers, and granddaughters worked together, often under the same roof. The older women taught the younger ones and the younger ones had babies to keep the circle of life going. This illness she suffered from was more bearable than the loneliness these thoughts triggered. She stood there, thousands of miles from home, from her Nan and from her mother's memory.

"May she rest in peace," she mumbled and did a hurried sign

of the cross. This was to be her new home. Her new Burren Bay. She coughed again, feeling the thick mucus in her lungs rattle.

Da's Uncle Patrick had first come to this area of the new world to survey for the Dominion of Canada. Whether homesick or just without imagination, he named it Burren Bay after the bay near his own home in Ireland. Now that she was here, she could see the similarities. The limestone pavements surrounding the lighthouse and extending back into the forest and down to the shoreline had the same pattern of crevices and boulders as the Burren back home. The cliffs, although not as high as the Cliffs of Moher, were still impressive as they towered over the bay. On a visit home, Uncle Patrick told her father about the opportunities in Canada.

"Joseph, it's a chance to get away from the land. Your wages are poor, and you will never own the land you're working," his uncle had said. The end of the Great Hunger had done little to pull their family out of poverty. They made ends meet, but just barely. They survived on potatoes and corn maize along with the odd egg or piece of mutton.

"But Mam is still with us. And Mary..." her father's voice was thick with heartache. Mary, her mother, had died when Oonagh was 6 years old, and her death was still raw for her father. He had to go on without her. He had to continue to provide for them. To parent her and her three brothers without the love of his life. Her father, she knew, was longing to escape his own loss and loneliness but leaving his mother and his beloved wife's remains would be difficult.

"Your Mam will be fine with your sisters. You need to think of your own family now. Mary would have wanted that. There's a lighthouse on Lake Huron on an island called Manitoulin. It's going to need a keeper come the spring. You should consider it Joseph. It would be ideal for the whole family, even little Oonagh. Promise me you'll think about this Joseph. An opportunity like this you'd never have in Ireland." Oonagh didn't see opportunity, only heartbreak having to leave her Nan.

She moved through the dining room and parlour. The furnishings were scant and worn. Everything would need a good washing or pounding to remove the dust and dirt of the winter. There was a root cellar outside that she would stock with the provisions they had brought with them from across the waters of the North Channel. Further deliveries from the mainland, they were told, would come by ship periodically through the summer and fall. Only a few things could be found in the tiny hamlet not far from the lighthouse. Their own personal belongings stacked outside with an old, worn steamer trunk were few. Aside from their clothing, her father brought tools and his Bible. Her brothers brought musical instruments—the timpan, fife, and flute. The art supplies she had carefully packed along with her oldest brother's music books had been lost at sea. Only a few pieces of charcoal Nan had made, and a couple of drawing tools had been saved. She had plans to make more once they were settled. But as she looked around the room there was much work to be done first.

"Now where would Nan start," she said aloud as her hand clutched the small burlap pouch that was hanging from a leather thong around her neck. The pouch and its contents had made her feel like Nan and her mother were right there with her throughout the whole journey to this new Burren Bay. She pulled the thong over her head, stuffing the pouch into her dress pocket. She removed her shawl and coat. It was time to get to work.

# CHAPTER 19

Norie felt sweat gather at the nape of her neck and trickle down her back as she leaned toward the fire Nell had built in the pit behind the tearoom. The evening was warm and the fire, warmer still. They were making charcoal from scratch and Norie had to admit to being interested in the whole process. After the soft launch and Canada Day celebrations the following day, time had stepped forward in Burren Bay with the repeated pattern of the circle of belonging at breakfast, lighthouse tours through the day, dinners in the late evening and fitful sleep into the darkest time of night. Burren Bay wasn't a busy place, but as a tourist destination, the number of visitors to the tearoom and museum was steadily increasing. Norie found herself moving through most days in a bit of a haze. Both tired and restless, her body and mind searched for something to ease the sameness and relieve the sorrow and melancholy that sat heavy in her limbs and organs. She was sometimes surprised at the physicality of her grief and anger.

"Well," Nell proclaimed as she stood over the steady flicker of flames, "There looks to be enough coals in the fire now to try."

From a plastic shopping-bag she brought with her, Nell handed Norie twigs cut from a variety of thin tree branches and vines, all about a quarter inch in diameter. Nell had gathered fallen apple and willow branches, twigs from Mountain Ash and maple trees. They all looked the same to Norie, at least initially. But as she stuffed them into an old, metal coffee can about six inches tall and four inches wide, she noticed they had different textures and smells. Nell explained that different trees would make different kinds of charcoal. While some would be soft, others would be harder, and they would all have their own unique overtones of blue, grey or brown. They were all roughly cut or broken to a uniform length with the bark removed. They were not dry twigs, but neither were they fresh and green. Once the can was filled, Nell fit the lid over the opening and tapped it into place with a hammer just like Norie had seen Grandma Johanna do with the lid of a paint can. With the lid firmly in place, the can would act like an oven to cook the wood. A hole Nell created in the lid with a hammer and nail would allow smoke, gases and steam to escape.

"It looked easy on the internet," Nell said, "So I'm pretty sure two confident, intelligent beings like us can do it." She laughed out loud. "The can eliminates the oxygen in the whole process so that the twigs will char instead of burn." With fire tongs she carefully nestled the can in the centre of the coals and flames.

Nell sat down on the log beside Norie. It was early evening, but the summer sun was still shining, and the air was warm. Wil was babysitting for one of the young mothers in the village and wouldn't be home until much later. Dahlia and Norie's mother were in the tearoom prepping for the next day. Norie and Alice had been avoiding each other for weeks, only being in the same space when they had no other choice. Dahlia assured her that her mother was sorry.

"If she could change things, Norie, she would." But those words felt hollow to Norie, and her anger and disappointment with her mother deepened. Norie and Nell sat together, quiet and thoughtful, gazing into the fire and watching.

"There we go...hear the steam starting to come out of the hole? And that flame is called a candle flame." Norie was amazed as moisture and gases blew out of the tiny hole. A narrow flame shot upwards, like a little torch on the top of the can. She wondered if the person who made the charcoal found in the tea tin had experienced the same amazement.

"The video I watched said it would take at least 30 minutes in the fire for the charcoal to form. We have to wait until the candle flame disappears." Nell leaned forward resting her elbows on her knees. They sat in silence for some time.

"So, have you worked much with charcoal?" Nell's voice interrupted the quiet.

"No," Norie lied. She had done a few assignments with commercial charcoal and hoped to do her final art project with the same medium. But that was before the accident.

"I love the gauzy nature of charcoal. Sometimes the image is right there on the page clear as day and other times the charcoal seems to obscure or veil the images."

"Sounds like you think the charcoal is doing the work without the artist's hand," Norie said.

"Don't you think there's another force at work when you create? Another deeper, more spiritual force?"

"I never thought of it like that." Norie paused, "I know that when I draw or paint it feels like everything stops around me. Like I leave the present."

"A lot of artists feel that way. I've read about dancers, musicians, writers, as well as visual artists talking about going into the zone.

It's like you don't hear or think or feel the world around you." Nell, who had been gazing into the fire, turned to look directly at Norie. "It's very therapeutic." Norie nodded, trying to get control of the tears that threatened to spill over her eyelashes.

They sat quietly for a few moments then Norie asked, "So you did the mural down on the wall of the general store?" Nell smiled. "I noticed the name *Cornelia* on the bottom of it and on the paintings you hung here. I shortened my name too."

"Yes, *Cornelia* is a hard name to live up to. What's your full name?"

"*Honora*," said Norie. "I really don't like it at all. I think it was my father's grandmother's name. My other grandma shortened it to Norie."

"*Honora* is a good name. I believe it means *woman of honour*. Mine means *horn*." They both laughed and then fell silent again.

"I think the time is up." Nell said and carefully removed the hot tin from the flames with the fire tongs, sitting it on the ground behind the log benches. "It has to cool completely before we can open it." They sat quietly beside each other waiting in the slow onset of mid-summer darkness, the light coming only from the windows of the tearoom kitchen and the fire before them.

Dahlia called from the back porch, "Would you two like a tumbler of lemonade?"

"Sounds wonderful Dahlia," Nell called as she stood up from the bench. "I think that charcoal's ready now, don't you?" She stepped over the log and very carefully tested the can. "It's nicely cooled. Norie, hand me that screwdriver." Norie retrieved the tool from the basket and Nell pried open the can. Inside, the twigs had transformed into charcoal. They were shrunken and curved, tinkling like glass beads when they rattled against each other and the sides of the tin. They were thin, black pieces of charcoal, just like the few pieces inside the tea tin she had found. Her budding interest was now full-fledged amazement. Nell handed her a piece and she rolled the stick in her fingertips. It was silky and smooth. No residue, just like the tea tin charcoal.

"How come it doesn't leave a mess on my fingers like the charcoal you buy in the store?"

"I think commercial charcoal is actually pressed charcoal powder. It's a little softer and that's what comes off on our hands. Commercial charcoal doesn't require a fixative though to keep it from smudging. This stuff will." She moved back across the log barrier to where her basket was and pulled out a few pieces of paper rolled up and tied with a ribbon.

"Come and sit," she invited Norie, as she unrolled the sheets of paper and clipped them to two clipboards. "I thought the best way to test this homemade charcoal was with parchment paper I made." The paper was heavier than sketchbook paper and felt textured and rough like cloth. Norie ran her hands over it to straighten and smooth it. Nell offered her a piece of charcoal. She hesitated, not wanting to put the charcoal to paper.

She was afraid. Afraid to create, as if her need to create wasn't the cause of all her heartache. Afraid to let herself go into that zone where only she mattered, and she would forget what had happened. Forget her grandmother. Forget the art box. Forget her father. Even forget her wounded mother. She didn't feel like she had the right to do that.

"I don't want to draw." Her voice was shaky and quiet.

Nell gazed at her for a moment and then taking Norie's hands in hers, she said, "We aren't drawing Norie. We are just testing the charcoal." Norie swallowed hard and took a few deep breaths. She looked at Nell and nodded.

The two worked the charcoal on the parchment paper, testing each piece of charcoal for colour and hardness. Some pieces created thin hard lines of black, while others lent themselves to soft, diaphanous lines. Thicker pieces of charcoal could be used flat on the paper to create wide swathes of shading. As Norie tested the sticks of charcoal, she felt herself relax and breathe more deeply than she had in months. Time became unmeasured as the two of them worked by the fire light. When Dahlia joined them with lemonade and cookies, Norie was surprised to find herself in the full darkness of night. Alice was nowhere to be seen.

"So," Dahlia asked, "How did the experiment go?"

"Famously, I would say," replied Nell. "It's remarkable how much variation there is in charcoal made from the different kinds of wood. I don't know that I would give up on the convenience of commercial charcoal, but I certainly like the change." Norie sketched lines and shapes with the charcoal, creating nothing in particular, just moving the blackened stick as an extension of her arm across the whiteness of the parchment. She felt free and light. She felt relief.

"You know, Norie," Dahlia said, "Your mother did some beautiful work with charcoal when she was studying art in university." Norie froze. Every cell of her body felt as if they were slamming into a wall.

"My mother," she stammered and started again, "My mother studied art?"

"Yes, of course," Dahlia looked confused, "You didn't know?"

"No," Norie put down the charcoal slowly and carefully, taking up the parchment in two hands. "Just another thing I didn't know."

She crumpled up the paper and threw it into the ebbing fire. The flames brightened for a moment then died down again. Norie stood and moved away from the fire, making her way around the house to the road, to the path to the lighthouse. As she rounded the corner of the house, she came face to face with Wil.

"What's up?" Wil asked surprised. Norie continued walking, unaware of the question, toward the lighthouse path. Nell and

Dahlia rounded the corner just behind Norie.

"Just let her be, Wil," Norie heard Dahlia say.

At the head of the path, she moved faster through the trees, knowing the path by heart now and feeling the urgency to get to the rock—to her sacred space, to her refuge. The breeze along the cliff cooled her fire-warmed skin as she staggered and lost her footing running along the loose stones. She forced herself to slow down, to move cautiously among the crevices and rocks. Just steps from the rock, when she was beginning to make out shapes and objects in the moonlight, she stopped short. Perched in her space was a girl around her own age, clothed in a long nightgown, a sketching board laid across her lap. The girl was unnaturally white, almost glowing in the moonlight and Norie blinked her eyes to be certain of what she was seeing as she slowly moved toward the stranger—a stranger Norie knew she had seen before.

"Who are you?" Norie finally asked when she was within reach of her. The girl gazed at Norie, not frightened or concerned. Norie felt her sadness. The girl spoke to her, but she couldn't understand what she was saying, her words distorted by a language Norie had never heard before—a dialect that sounded ancient. Norie focused on her lips, on her jaw and her throat, trying to make sense of the sounds she heard. Her gaze slipped down toward a pouch hanging around the girl's neck and she gasped, her hand rising instinctively to the pouch around her own neck. When Norie took one more step toward the apparition, she disappeared. The rock, her refuge, once again sat empty.

# CHAPTER 20

Norie held the open tea tin on her lap, its contents splayed across the cot. She felt damp and sweaty even though she had been awake for a while, already showered and dressed. It was the hottest morning in the stuffy attic since coming to Burren Bay. The fan was busily spinning, but unless you sat right in front of it, the cooling effect was lost. She placed the pouch on her pillow, setting it apart from the other items. It was identical to the pouch around the neck of the girl she encountered at her rock the night before, although now it showed the ravages of time with missing beads and charcoal staining on the leather—like the girl herself seemingly from another place and time. Her eyes travelled across the blanket to the leather stump and feather, to the charcoal. She caressed the delicate pieces, recalling through the nerves of her fingertips, the smoothness of the charcoal she helped to create the night before. Picking up a piece, she examined it more closely. It was long and thin, from a willow bush perhaps, she didn't really know, but it looked like some of the twigs she and Nell had cooked. In her fingers it felt as light as a feather, and her hands recalled the sensation of the charcoal sliding across the parchment as she tested the various pieces. It felt good to hold on to it.

She reached into her backpack and pulled out the two sketches she had found in the lighthouse storeroom. Sharp clear lines of charcoal outlined the cliff edge and the framing of the lighthouse. She imagined the artist softening the charred blackness of the trees with feathers. She knew that the patches of clean cream paper butting up against spaces of misty charcoal were created by erasing charcoal already laid down. The effect was mysterious.

"Are you okay?" She startled at Wil's voice. "Sorry, didn't mean to scare you. It's just, my mom told me what happened, what upset you last night. I also overheard my mom talking to your mom. Well, it was mostly my mom talking and your mom crying." Norie sighed. "She really feels bad, you know. I heard her tell Mom that it was all her fault. That she should have told you stuff. That you weren't a baby anymore." Norie gathered the items on her bed and replaced them in the tea tin. The pouch of stones she clutched in her hands.

"Girls...breakfast is ready!" Dahlia's voice called from the kitchen.

"Coming Mom!" Wil called back. She pulled on her shorts and t-shirt and ran her fingers through her hair. "Are you coming?" she asked, glancing at Norie who was still sitting on her cot. As Wil moved ahead of her on the stairs, Norie hung the pouch around her neck, again secreting it under her t-shirt.

At the bottom of the stairs Wil turned left into the washroom as Norie turned right and continued toward the kitchen. She and Gibson almost collided at the corner into the dining room.

"Oh," Norie was startled. "Sorry."

"It's okay," returned Gibson. "I'm just getting Dahlia's agenda from the office." He stood aside to let Norie pass. She hesitated then spoke.

"I have to apologize to you, Gibson." She paused to steady her breathing. "I was so rude the other day. I had no idea about anything you've ever gone through in your life, and I had no right judging you the way I did." Gibson nodded and smiled.

"Thank you Norie. I really appreciate your apology. I know you've been through something horrible, but everyone here has your best interests in mind. If you need anything, anything at all, just ask. Even if it's just to talk."

"I will," she answered. "I promise, I will. And—" she hesitated, embarrassed by her awkwardness, "I'm sorry for your loss."

"Thank you Norie. I'm sorry for your loss as well." She nodded and moved on toward the kitchen.

Alice was not in the kitchen that morning when Dahlia invited them to join hands for the circle of belonging. Without her mother present at the table, the four of them had to reach out to each other to cover the gap where her mother usually sat. Gibson reached his hand across the table towards Norie to close the circle. Hesitant at first, she glanced at Wil. Wil nodded and Norie took Gibson's hand. The circle of belonging closed and Dahlia proceeded with the prayer. Afterwards, she served fresh tea biscuits and homemade jellies, a morning staple, alongside hot tea she had blended herself.

"Drink it up while it's hot," Dahlia said, "Because it will be iced tea by this afternoon. Today is supposed to be a scorcher. Could be a busy day."

It was not. Norie and Wil spent the first part of the morning dusting and tidying, keeping themselves busy in between a very slow trickle of visitors. By midmorning the lighthouse museum was hot and stuffy, and Wil coaxed a few old windows open allowing the breeze picking up along the cliff edge to creep in, moving air around the otherwise airless rooms. Norie couldn't sit still as she perched on the edge of the stool behind the entrance desk. An old office fan oscillated in the corner, keeping the entranceway cool, but Norie was agitated. She jumped up repeatedly to tidy the brochure display, straighten old, framed photos on the wall, and sweep the entrance. She sorted and counted coins in the cash box. She cleaned the glass door of the display case. When there were no jobs left to do, she absentmindedly picked up a pencil and started to doodle on a note pad the girls kept on the counter.

She printed her name in small, precise letters. Norie Lynch. Neat and tidy. Legible and clean. Then she wrote it in large, two-dimensional block capitals, extending lines and shading in spaces to create a three-dimensional effect. As she worked, she thought about her favourite colours and how, if she had pencil crayons with her, she would colour in each letter. The *N* and *E* would be coloured in a solid green, framing her name, while the other letters would be decorated with patterns of dots and lines. She practised her signature, something she started doing when she first realized that artists always sign their work. In the beginning she perfected *Honora*, her given name, but as she got older, she preferred the shortened version and so refined how she wrote *Norie* cursively. She imagined signing her work, signing autographs and signing contracts all as a famous, successful artist. She switched to a clean piece of paper and drew the little landscape sketches she had perfected, practiced over and over again—the ones her classmates and teachers had praised, the ones she developed in art class using what she learned about line, shape, texture, shading.

"Wow," said Wil, "You've been busy!" Norie looked up at Wil, her mind having shifted from the playful meandering of doodling to the focused thinking of drawing and creating art. Pieces of paper were strewn across the counter, a few having floated off and been blown up against the display cabinet by the fan. Wil bent over and picked up a few sheets. She looked back at Norie with amazement.

"You are really good!"

Norie quickly collected the papers. "They're just doodles. Did you want something?" her voice, tight.

"It's lunch time." The hour and a half since she last looked at the clock had flown. Her hands shook as she collected the sheets that fell to the floor closest to her. Wil helped her pick up the papers gazing thoughtfully at each one. "My doodling doesn't look anything like this." She held up a drawing of a small rowboat tied to an old wooden dock. There was a cabin in the distance, sitting along a river's edge. "My doodles are squiggles and shapes. Just marks on a page. This is drawing, Norie." She held up the landscape. "This is a work of art."

Norie grabbed the piece of paper from Wil's hands. The calmness she felt, the timelessness she had been experiencing, was gone. Now all her fears and pain seemed to return tenfold. She moved ahead of Wil and out the door of the lighthouse. She marched back to the tearoom aware of Wil following close behind. When she got to the cottage, she made her way to the back yard. There, sitting before the cold fire pit, she crumpled every piece of paper into balls and threw them into the blackened remains of the last fire. Then, with the poker, she pushed each ball into the cold ashes until they were unrecognizable. She got up and walked past Wil, who had been standing at the corner of the house watching, and asked, "Are you coming in for lunch?"

Much later, as night began to fall, Norie sat at the edge of the fire pit gazing into the blackness. She had to finish her work from lunch. She was going to set fire to the crumpled balls of paper she had buried in the coals. She could hear the muffled noise of Dahlia, Gibson and Wil playing Scrabble in the cottage. Alice had made an appearance at dinner time, pushed food around her plate for twenty minutes and then excused herself to return to her bedroom. Probably for the night. Unable to understand her mother, Norie focused on the scrunched-up wads of paper buried under the ash. She added kindling and newspaper to the pit, arranging it like Nell had done the night they made charcoal. Finally, she stacked small logs on top of it all.

She didn't really think doodling alone represented her art in the truest sense of the word. Doodling was mindless—a stream of consciousness exercise. It calmed her and occupied her mind while she did it. She couldn't even remember what she had been thinking about during the hours she spent doodling at the counter in the lighthouse. She planned nothing. She allowed her mind to wander visually on paper, playing with the elements of design. Doodling was like stretching before going for a run or warming up your vocal cords before singing. She was completely certain the instant Wil brought her attention back to the real world, that doodling would eventually lead her to drawing and drawing would inspire her need to create art. And that need, she had learned the hard way, led to loss.

She struck the match and lit the corner of the newspaper closest to her. The paper ignited, the fire moving in a circle around the firepit burning tentatively and then flaring up with brightness and heat.

"So, you finished the job off, did you?" Norie glanced up at Wil.

"Yup."

"I guess all artists have moments like this." Wil sat down beside Norie.

"What do you mean?"

"Well...who's the old guy who painted all the water lilies?"

"You mean Monet?"

"Right...well he destroyed a bunch of his own paintings. He thought they weren't as good as some of his others, so he destroyed them." Norie stared into the flames as the larger pieces of wood began to catch fire. "All you artist types are so hard on yourselves."

"Maybe, but maybe for good reason," Norie said.

"Or maybe you are all just being too dramatic." Norie turned to Wil, ready to defend herself, to defend Monet, but Wil raised her hands to stop her. "Look Norie, I know what happened to you, losing your father and having to watch your mother struggle like this, has been difficult. But do you really think that giving up drawing is going to keep anything bad from happening ever again? That doesn't make any sense." Wil's voice had gotten louder as she spoke, and Norie stood to defend herself.

"Well, maybe sprinkling biscuit crumbs on windowsills doesn't make any sense either, but you guys still do that." Wil stood to meet her face to face.

"But sprinkling crumbs hurts no one Norie. It doesn't hurt me or my mother or you or anyone. Burning your own work in a firepit is hurtful. It's hurting you." The two girls looked at each other intently. Finally, Norie turned away and sat down, spent. Wil returned to her seat beside her.

"I'm sorry. I shouldn't have even brought it up."

"No," said Norie, "You're right." She sighed. "I just don't know what to do. When I was doodling today, in the lighthouse, it felt so good to forget everything for a while. Then when I did remember, it felt like I was, I don't know, too happy."

"It's okay to feel happy or at least not sad. You don't have to mourn every minute of the day. If you can forget everything you've had to live through lately for a little while when you draw, then do it." Wil paused. "I don't approve of the fact that my father left us. He just got up and walked away. When I really dwell on it, it makes me angry and lonely all at the same time. But I don't have to pretend he doesn't exist or that he was someone he wasn't. My parents' marriage fell apart and it doesn't matter whose fault it was. I know stuff went on that I had no idea about. I don't need to know all the family secrets."

"You make it sound so simple," Norie said.

"It's not simple. So, don't give up on everything because of this one thing in your life. It sucks but it happened without you wanting it to. Don't purposefully cause any more tragedy."

Norie glanced at the fire, the balled-up paper gone now, burnt to ash. "They were good fire-starting doodles though." And the two girls laughed.

# CHAPTER 21

*Grosse Ile, Quebec, April 1892*

Their arrival at Grosse Ile was marked with an overwhelming sense of relief. It was a godsend to be allowed out of the dark and smelly confines of steerage into the sunlight and fresh air. It had been a rough voyage, bad weather and harsh seas for most of the crossing. Access to the upper deck had been severely limited for everyone and once she started to have symptoms of lung sickness, Oonagh was kept in her bunk, unable to move around even below deck. At least she had made it to Canada in one piece. They had arrived together.

The light hurt her eyes as she was lifted to the upper deck. She was weak but managed to stand supported by her father. The smells of unwashed bodies and toilet rooms that had been poorly maintained during the last days of the trip were replaced with salty air and fish. They were herded off the ship and onto a pier where a long line of passengers was forming. It wound forward toward clerks who would collect their personal information and then onto medical inspections. Oonagh placed her hand on her chest as a deep, wracking cough came on suddenly. She could feel the pouch Nan had given her secure around her neck. Her father and brothers fought to stay in a tight group as they were moved along the pier to solid ground, to Canadian soil. The boys carried all their belongings while her father attended to Oonagh as she tried to regain the ability to walk normally on solid ground. Check point after check point, they moved toward the long houses where the passengers, now officially immigrants, sat and waited for instructions. She was exhausted by the time they sat down on a long, low-lying wooden bench. Gazing up at her father, his hair and beard ragged and dirty, she realized how difficult this trip had been on him. They had made it this far together, but they were all physically and emotionally overwhelmed.

A young woman dressed all in white, a scarf holding back her hair, moved among the arrivals, examining the very young and the infirmed. Those who even Oonagh could tell were gravely ill were carried away to the hospital building for immediate care. One young mother tried to follow when her child was scooped up, but her husband held her back while the woman in white spoke softly and reassuringly to her. The young woman wept quietly burying her face in her hands. Eventually, the woman in white was standing in front of Oonagh.

"Well, who have we here? A young lass from across the pond?" Her smile was warm as were her hands as she felt Oonagh's forehead and examined along her jawline, behind her ears and along her neck. "Haven't been feeling well, love?"

"She's had a nasty cough," explained her father, "With some fever on and off for a few days now. And she's tired to the bone." Her father's voice startled her. His words were almost whispered, each one heavy and brittle.

"Well let's get this fine lass moved to the hospital so Dr. Whitgale can take a look at her." An orderly standing behind the nurse, came forward to help Oonagh to the doorway. Her father moved to follow, but the nurse put her hand on his arm. "You need to stay here with the rest of your family to clear quarantine. She will be in good hands. Someone will come and fetch you later." Her father nodded and gently handed her over to the orderly. Oonagh looked up at him.

"It will be okay, Da," she smiled and allowed the orderly to guide her to the doorway.

Oonagh couldn't remember much of those first few days in the hospital except a flurry of activity—being bathed and clothed in fresh linens, encouraged to drink and eat. One evening, as she began to spend more time awake than asleep, Oonagh listened as an older nurse, perhaps her father's age, scoffed at Dr. Whitgale's new fandangle treatment for consumption.

"He prefers to stuff his patients full of chemicals rather than sending them off to sanitariums in the countryside. We've done it for years and now it's not good enough somehow." The young nurse who she had first seen in the long house, assuaged her.

"Nurse, you know he's studied at the finest institutes. He truly knows what's best."

"Oh yes, these new doctors always know what's best."

"Where is my family?" Oonagh interrupted.

"Sweet girl, don't you worry about your family. They are all being well cared for," said the young nurse.

"Yes, poppet, you just lie back and let us worry about things."

That was the last she remembered until she woke to find her father, clean, his beard and hair freshly trimmed, sitting by her bedside.

"I didn't think you would ever wake up lass," he teased, and she smiled back. He stood to kiss her on the very top of her head.

"When do we leave from here," she asked. "No one has said a thing to me. What have they told you?" She took a long breath after speaking so many words in one go. She began to cough until she spit up in a cloth the nurse had given her. Her father helped her to lie back against the pillows again until the spasm in her chest subsided.

"It's going to be a few days yet before we can take you with us. I've been in touch with Uncle Patrick. He's trying to arrange passage for us to Toronto and then further north to the lighthouse. But we have to wait for you to be a little stronger before we can leave." Her father paused, closing his eyes for a moment, taking a heavy breath.

"What is it Da? What's wrong with me? Am I—am I going to die?" The word frightened her. She had already lost so much. To come this far just to die would be unbearable.

"No, no child. You are not going to die." She relaxed into her pillow. She placed her hand on her chest reassuring herself that the pouch was still there. The nurse who had tended her when she first arrived took it and promised to clean it and return it to her, which she did. Everything was more bearable with her little pouch of stones around her neck. Nan had made sure of that.

"But you are very sick." Her father continued, "The doctor says you have consumption, phthisis I think they call it. He's giving you some medicine and he believes that rest and lots of fresh air and exercise will help too. He thinks that if we can make it to the Burren Bay Lighthouse, it may just be the right place for you to get better. Uncle Patrick is doing his best to get us there by month's end."

"How are the boys? Are they with you? Can they come visit me?"

"The boys are fine. We are all waiting here together until we hear from Patrick." Then he lowered his eyes, staring at his hand. "But I do have to tell you something."

"What? Tell me Da. Tell me!" Her voice cracked and she began to cough again. When the cough subsided Oonagh implored weekly. "What happened, Da?"

She watched her father's brow wrinkle and jaw tighten at the thought of causing her more concern. He took her hands in his as he spoke softly.

"Some of our belongings didn't make it to shore. A couple of bags were lost at sea or misplaced when we boarded. I don't know how or when. But..." He paused.

"Not my art supplies?" He looked up at her and then back to his hands again. She felt her heart crack, just a little. Nan had gathered supplies for her for weeks leading up to their departure. Her grandfather had made a whole batch of new charcoal. She and Nan had worked for days making paper and collecting feathers and bits of leather and twine to make stumps. Now it was all gone.

"I'm so sorry." Then he added, "We did save the little sack you had with the few things you brought on board to pass the time." He picked up a bundle from the floor beside the chair he had been sitting on. "I think there were a few supplies in there, weren't there? The bag got destroyed during decontamination, but I wrapped it all in a handkerchief." He laid the bundle on the foot of her cot and opened the flaps. There were a few sticks of charcoal, a feather and a leather stump laying in the pile. She gazed at the remains of her supplies, one tear silently rolling down her cheek. Her father wiped it away with rough hands.

"We'll see if Uncle Patrick can get you some more." He paused, "But for now you need to rest and get stronger for our journey." He got up to leave as the young nurse approached the bed to attend to Oonagh.

"Da?"

"Yes, Oonagh?"

"Thank you."

"You are welcome, my little treasure," he murmured into her hair as he hugged her tightly.

The nurse stood back as Oonagh and her father said their goodbyes. She smiled at Oonagh and looked down at the cloth and its contents.

"You know," she said, "There's an empty tea tin in the kitchen. I could see if Cook is willing to part with it."

"They're just a few art supplies," said Oonagh.

"Even a few art supplies need a proper container."

Late in the night Oonagh awoke in a fit of coughing. She sat up hacking into the spitting cloth until the spell was over. As she reached to put the soiled cloth on the small table beside her bed, she noticed a square tea tin, bright yellow with a red ribbon painted onto it. She picked it up, remembering that the nurse had promised to retrieve the tin for her art supplies. She pulled off the lid and mingled with the scent of orange pekoe tea, was the pungent odour of charcoal and leather. She picked out a piece of charcoal, placing the tin on the bed between her knees. It felt smooth and hard. "As strong as a nail," Nan had said. She put it to her nose and breathed in the charcoal's aroma. It was a little bit of home, and it comforted her. Smiling, she put the charcoal back in the tin, pushed the lid on and placed it on the little table. It wasn't long before she was in a sound sleep.

# CHAPTER 22

Norie sat staring out the kitchen window. The chickadees and sparrows who fed each morning seemed to have brought their extended families with them that day. A dozen or so birds took turns flying between an old bird bath in the middle of the yard and the window where they pecked at tiny morsels of fennel biscuits sprinkled along the sill. Several hummingbirds fought for position on the two feeders Dahlia hung on a tree nearby. They flitted amongst the leaves of the tree, aggressively chirping and flying at each other, the males protecting their territory, the females protecting their young.

"The weather report is calling for a storm later today, but it's beautiful right now," said Dahlia as she followed Norie's gaze out the window.

"It's too hot," complained Wil. "They've been calling for a storm now for days. All it does is get hotter and stickier, clouds roll in and then right back out. I'll believe it when I see it."

"Can't always believe the weatherman, kiddo," joked Gibson as he lifted the tea tray to the table.

"Good morning."

Norie looked up as her mother made her first appearance at breakfast since her apology.

"Good morning," said Dahlia, unable to hide her surprise. "Happy to see you so early in the morning. Wilhelmina, get Alice a cup of tea." Wil obliged her mother while pulling a questioning face only Norie could see. Alice was dressed in denim capris and a tank top, her hair cut shorter than Norie had ever seen it. She was a little pale but clean and tidy. Most of her injuries were now bright angry scars, only a few lightly bandaged. Norie was again surprised at how she had simply abandoned taking care of her mother's wounds once they arrived at Burren Bay. She supposed Dahlia had taken over, but she wasn't sure. Maybe her mother had taken responsibility for her own care. Norie's stomach tightened at the thought of how easily she ditched her mother. Maybe they were more alike than she imagined.

Alice nodded at Norie, and she nodded back. Dahlia placed a plate of fresh baking on the table and sat down reaching for the hands of Wil and Alice sitting immediately beside her. Gibson took Wil's hand and Wil took Norie's. Alice stretched her hand across the table toward Norie. Norie hesitated, gazing at her mother's fingers, long and bony, unfamiliar. She was reluctant to hold them. Dahlia cleared her throat as if to begin the circle of belonging prayer. Wil encouraged Norie with wide eyes and a quick nod. Norie took her mother's hand in her own and Dahlia began.

> "Circle us, keep hope within, and despair without.
> Circle us, keep peace within, and worry without.
> Circle us, keep love within, and hatred without.
> Circle us, keep courage within, and fear without.

Circle us, keep light within, and darkness without."

As soon as Dahlia finished, Norie let go of Alice's hand. Her palm felt warm and clammy, and she rubbed it on her shorts under the table. With her other hand she felt for the pouch under her shirt. The stones reminded her to breathe.

During breakfast Norie was painfully aware of her mother. She seemed calm and relaxed, unlike what Norie had witnessed over the last month. It was as if she had worked through some of her grief and was, for now anyway, at peace with herself. While Norie ate scones and sipped tea, her mother and Dahlia made plans for the day in the tearoom. When she and Wil finished eating, they cleared the table and did the dishes. As they started to leave to go to work at the lighthouse Alice spoke to Norie.

"If you have a minute, Norie, before you go to the lighthouse, I have something I want to give you." Norie stopped and waited at the kitchen doorway until her mother got up and made her way to her bedroom. Norie followed and stood in the bedroom doorway while her mother retrieved a package from the nightstand drawer.

"This is for you," she said, handing a small package to Norie. It was wrapped in brown paper and was the size of a paperback or small frame. "It's just, well given everything that's happened, it's just something I want you to have." Norie took the package in her hand. She didn't know what to say. "But don't open it until you're alone. It's kind of private. Between you and me." Her mother smiled tightly.

"Thanks," said Norie as her mother turned away from her and sat on the edge of the bed, her face in her hands. Norie left the tearoom quietly. She walked toward the lighthouse not attending to anything around her except the weight of the parcel she had clutched in her hands. Wil met her at the edge of the pathway.

"What was that all about?" Wil leaned her head towards Norie, eyes wide with curiosity. "What's in the package?"

"I have no idea," responded Norie. She turned the parcel over in her hands. She wanted to open it, right then and there, but given everything that had happened since their arrival to Burren Bay, Norie wasn't sure if she really wanted to know what it was.

"Are you going to open it?" Wil asked.

"She said to open it when I'm by myself. She said it was private." Norie looked at Wil as her face fell. "I'll tell you what it is, I promise. But I think I'm going to open it alone first. I don't know what it is."

"Are you going back to our room?" Wil asked.

"No, I think the best place for this is my rock. I won't be long." She hoped. The two girls made their way through the treed pathway. When they reached the alvar pavement, Norie moved off toward the stand of trees to the right. Toward her rock. She hadn't seen the mysterious girl in days, but she always felt her comforting presence. Her rock was the place she had come to feel most safe. She watched as Wil reached the lighthouse and looked back at her and waved. She waved back and then sat on the rock, pushing herself backward into the trees, under cover. She had become accustomed to the feeling of the rock—its ridges and crevices familiar to her skin and muscles. The gentle scratching of tree branches across her bare arms was pleasant and distracting. Today the light breeze along the cliff that cooled her skin stopped outside the copse of trees that surrounded her. She sat, legs crossed and looked at the parcel her mother had gifted her.

The brown butcher paper was neatly creased at the edges and the whole package was tied with string. Norie untied the bow holding it all together and the paper fell away. Inside was a small, framed picture. It was a pencil sketch of a little girl, 2 or 3-years-old, playing in a yard surrounded by flowers and trees. As Norie examined the drawing, she could see the techniques the artist used to create the scene. She could almost feel the artist's pencil in her own hand. Fine thin lines created the little figure, her curls, her dress, the edge of her face. Loose lines, some dark and hard, others thin and light, created the garden around the little girl. Flower upon flower blended into long grass and bushes. Small circles hinted at the petals on roses closest to the eye. Stippling created faded foot paths along the outer edge of the drawing. There was something familiar about this scene, something she couldn't quite put her finger on. She turned over the frame and found a folded note taped to the back. She recognized her mother's writing instantly.

*Norie,*
*This is a little drawing of you when you were a toddler at Grandma Johanna's house, in the garden in June. You were such a carefree little girl. It breaks my heart knowing what you've gone through these last months. I apologize for that. I realize now how my actions, your father's actions too, have hurt you. I want you to have this little sketch, my most treasured belonging, as a sign of my love regardless of the mistakes I've made.*
*Mom.*

Now she remembered. The rose garden. The path to the potting shed. The trees that framed the back of the lot. Norie had many warm memories of being a little girl at Grandma Johanna's house. She closed her eyes and remembered that garden—running through the sprinkler on a hot summer day, the smell of freshly cut grass, ice-cold lemonade on a bright August afternoon. She had so few memories of her Grandpa Jack. He had died when she was quite young. But Grandma Johanna was a strong presence during her whole life. Even after she fell sick and her house was sold, and she moved to the nursing home, Grandma Johanna was always there for her. The pain of losing the drawing box sharpened in Norie's heart. Flipping the picture over again, she lost herself in the few memories she had of that time. They were happy memories, unblemished by anger and disappointment. A time before guilt and grief sat heavy in her chest like a boulder, weighing her down and making it difficult to breathe. A lump formed in her throat and tears threatened to spill onto her mother's note in her hands.

Blinking them back, Norie flipped the frame around to gaze again at the picture. She remembered seeing some of her grandmother's sketches hanging in her home. It was those sketches that so inspired Norie as the heir to the family's talent. However, she didn't recall ever seeing this sketch. In the bottom right hand corner she noticed the signature. Small, loopy, even strokes slanting slightly to the left. The initial letters of both the first and last name carefully curled around the remaining letters as if protecting them. And then it dawned on her. This was her mother's signature. The artist's hand that she saw and felt so clearly was her mother's. And then there was no stopping the tears.

# CHAPTER 23

Forty-five minutes later, Norie arrived at the lighthouse. The breeze picking up along the cliff cooled her hot skin. She looked out across the bay at the water churning in the strengthening wind. The Burren Bay sketches she found weeks ago, flashed through her mind and, for a moment, she had the urge to capture the scene in front of her on paper. She stopped and scanned the horizon. Not a cloud in sight. Maybe later, she thought, still hesitant to put charcoal to paper. She turned back to the lighthouse. With swollen eyes and a runny nose, she knew Wil would have questions.

"Oh my God! Are you alright?" Wil asked.

"Actually yes," replied Norie. It was a quiet morning, so Norie took her time explaining.

"So, your mom gave you a drawing that she did. I didn't see that coming!"

"Me neither," agreed Norie.

"Are you going to be alright?" Norie nodded.

"I can't say I feel great, but I don't have a headache anymore." She smiled at Wil. "Am I on the counter again today?"

"Yup. I've just started the dusting, so I'll finish that up before lunch." The two girls kept busy in between the handful of people who visited the lighthouse that morning. Norie tidied tourism brochures and restocked the shelf of sale items. They had started selling Nell's postcards and prints, local history books written by Island authors and a few other craft items over the last few weeks. Dahlia thought it would be a way of generating funds and supporting local artists, writers and crafters. They didn't sell much, but it made the counter area a little more interesting.

As Norie straightened the pile of books in front of her, she thought about the drawing her mother had given her. She had no idea if the little sketch of her as a toddler was the last thing her mother had done, but she was curious about whether other pieces existed. For some reason her mother had completely given up her art. What could have happened to make Alice walk away from something she clearly loved and excelled at—give up something she had gone to school to study? Norie stopped, her hands frozen on the pile of books she had been straightening, aligning the spines, pushing their edges even with each other to form a neat, symmetrical stack. What was she thinking? Of course, she could understand her mother's actions. Hadn't she done the same thing? The door of the lighthouse banged open and a family of five fell through it. Norie left her thoughts as she began her lighthouse spiel.

The girls had lunch at the tearoom. Dahlia sat them at a corner table in the front room and served them along with four or five other groups who were having lunch before touring the lighthouse. Alice was working in the kitchen, so Norie did not get to thank her for the sketch. She was relieved because she didn't know what to say anyway. After they ate, Wil returned to the lighthouse right away, while Norie took a moment to tuck the gift in her bag upstairs in their bedroom. She pulled out the two sketches of Burren Bay—her Burren Bay. For the first time since before the accident she could feel the strong urge to draw. It was as much a neurological urge as an emotional one. It started in her brain and swiftly transmitted down her spine and into the nerves of her arms, hands and fingers. It was like an itch that needed scratching and it both excited and frightened her. For a long time, she had seen this urge as the cause of everything bad that had happened. Now she wasn't certain. She heard voices and movement as some of the tearoom guests were readying to leave. She hurried to catch up with Wil for a busy afternoon.

And a busy afternoon it was. The heat and wind didn't keep people away. Norie guessed they were enjoying stretches in their air-conditioned cars as they toured the Island making their way from sight to sight. Finally, as the last group of women left the lighthouse at closing, Wil and Norie sat in the shade outside the porch leading to the main entrance. Here they escaped the searing sun but had the benefit of the wind blowing over them to keep them cool. A very distant rumble could be heard over the increasing wave action in the bay.

"Is that thunder?" Norie had been wondering the same thing. "Probably another fake storm coming in," mused Wil. "Everything is so parched. We could use a good downpour."

"If it rains, I swear I'll go out and stand in it." Norie felt grimy and sweaty.

"Have you seen your mom today yet? I mean to talk about the gift she gave you?"

"No," replied Norie. "I was hoping maybe later tonight. It was too busy today." Besides, she thought to herself, I'm not quite sure what to say yet. "Let's go back to see what's for dinner. Not that I feel like eating in this heat." Wil agreed as they locked up the lighthouse and headed back to the tearoom.

Alice did not come out of her room for dinner.

"Your mom is resting. I exhausted her today, I think," Dahlia explained away Alice's absence. Norie was relieved. Now she had a little more time to plan her words carefully before approaching her mother. Dahlia glanced out the kitchen window. Gibson had gone into town to help Mrs. Kingstown put her lawn furniture in her shed. Norie noticed the birds were absent this evening. The hummingbirds typically flew in at the end of the afternoon for one last battle for sugared water. They were suspiciously absent, perhaps tucked safely away from the impending storm. "There are some ominous dark clouds moving in. Did you batten down the hatches at the lighthouse?"

"We locked up," assured Wil, and then she added, "Should we have closed the shutters?"

"Probably wouldn't be a bad idea," agreed Dahlia.

"I'll go Wil. You stay and help your mom. There are only three sets of shutters anyway. Besides, there's something I want to do." Norie left the kitchen before Dahlia or Wil could ask what she meant. She ran up to the attic bedroom and dumped out some of the contents of her backpack on her cot. She placed her mother's sketch on her pillow—a place of honour and safe keeping. She tucked the sketch pad Dahlia had given her the first days in Burren Bay into the bag. She also grabbed the tea tin and a couple of extra pieces of charcoal that she and Nell had made. Her hand instinctively brushed the pouch hanging around her neck.

Breathe. The word resounded in her brain as if a stranger's voice had gained access to her thoughts. Breathe. She threw the strap of her backpack over her shoulder and headed downstairs.

Quickly she made her way down the path, into the trees and out onto the lighthouse cliff. The wind was considerably stronger than it had been just a couple of hours earlier. Maybe this would be the big storm the meteorologists were predicting. Black clouds sat at the opening of the bay, and the distant rumbling was a little louder now. It certainly didn't sound or look like a fake storm. Norie put both her arms through the backpack straps and quickly made her way to the lighthouse to close and lock the shutters. It was harder than she thought it would be, but fortunately two of three sets of shutters were on the opposite side of the building, sheltered from the brunt of the wind. When she was done, she made her way to the rock, her sacred space, and tucked herself inside the opening. From this vantage point she had a wide-open view of the lighthouse and the bay, like the view from the sketches. The trees that surrounded her moved only slightly in the wind— their branches tangled tightly amongst each other. She took out the sketch pad and a piece of charcoal from the tin. For a moment everything seemed to grow quiet, as if another force was forming a bubble around her space. And then Norie saw her.

The girl stood about fifteen feet in front of her looking squarely at Norie. Her long hair and nightdress blew wildly in the wind, but she stood her ground. Her face was serene, and she nodded at Norie. Norie looked down at the blank page of the sketchpad resting on her lap. She took deep cleansing breaths. The warm, moist air soothed her nose, mouth, and throat, and bathed her lungs. Then, picking up a piece of charcoal she began to draw.

# CHAPTER 24

## County Clare, Ireland, March 1892

The bullish wind pushed them along the cow trail at the bottom of the cliff. Oonagh and her grandmother walked daily along this path on the edge of the farm along the shore of a little bay they called Burren Bay. They gathered their shawls around their shoulders and woollen hoods to their heads to fend off the early spring weather. Like most March days, it was cool, wet, and windy on the farm, but never more so than at this edge of Ireland where the rocky cliffs met the Atlantic Ocean. Oonagh could tell the old woman was growing tired of their walk, their last before she and her brothers and father left for Canada. She was old enough now to know what leaving home meant. Once she left, Oonagh would never see her Nan again.

"Oonagh," her grandmother called over the wind, "Give me your arm, *cailin*, to steady my old feet." The old woman waddled along the rough path, her feet squeezed by the new brogues Uncle Patrick had sent her from the city. Oonagh had rubbed her old feet with nettle leaf and bees' wax ointment just last night. Since she was a small child, she loved to rub Nan's feet. It was an intimate gesture that bound the two generations. Her grandmother had been a surrogate mother after her own dear Mam had passed. Nan made certain that Oonagh knew everything about her mother—how she sang while she worked, how her long, red hair curled in tendrils around her fair face, how her smile brightened everyone's day. Oonagh was just like her, or so her grandmother told her, except for her own long black locks.

She had her Mam's talent for drawing too. Whenever she could, Oonagh sketched the land around her—the farmhouse, the paddocks, the sheep, the landscape across the Burren. Often, she would hike to the top of the very trail they followed now and sketch the wide expanse of the bay. Over the last few weeks, since their departure date had been set, Oonagh had tried to capture on paper this place she had known as home her whole life. A place she may never, ever see again once they sailed. Her grandparents made sure she was leaving with enough supplies to keep her sketching in her new country. But she couldn't believe that Canada was as beautiful as her own Burren Bay.

She felt her grandmother's weight pull against her arm.

"Let's sit for a moment, Nan," encouraged Oonagh. "We can rest a bit on this wall and then head back home, and I'll make you some nice hot tea." Her grandmother sat heavily on the stone sighing with relief when she took the weight off her feet. Oonagh plopped herself down beside her. "What I am going to do without you Nan," she moaned. "How will I learn to bake bread or know when the *colcannon* and *stobhach* are done? Who will teach me about stitching and darning? Who will help me make charcoal and paper?"

"My girl, you've learned all you need to know to take care

of your father and brothers. You don't need me to teach you anymore." She squeezed Oonagh's arm. "This is going to be your grand adventure, Oonagh! A chance to go somewhere most of us have never gone."

"I don't want an adventure without you Nan," she replied. "I'll be all alone. One girl among all those men." Even her youngest brother was old enough to do the work of a man.

"Oonagh, you will always be a part of the womenfolk of this family, even far away in Canada. Let me show you." The old woman shifted her weight on the wall and bent over to pick up something off the ground. "Look at these three stones, Oonagh. They are all different, are they not?" The three stones her grandmother held in the palm of her hand were fragments of the limestone rock along the edge of the Burren. One was as white as bone from laying exposed to the sun, its edges made smooth by wind and water. The second had a small fossil embedded in its centre. The third had blackened with age and exposure to the air. "They're all different and unique. Aren't they?" Oonagh nodded in agreement. "But they are all from the same Burren stone that our family has lived on for generations. Many died on this Burren karst, but many survived too. All in their own way and in their own time."

"This black one is me, old and dark," she laughed as she said it. "This one here," she said pointing to the stone with the fossil. "This one is your mother. That piece of bone inside it is her heart. It represents all the love she left behind for us." Oonagh took the last stone in her own fingers. "That one is you, Oonagh. White as bone, fresh and young and smooth." Nan put the other two stones in Oonagh's hand, enclosing them in her fingers. "These three stones represent our lineage, our traditions, our history. If you carry them with you to Canada, then you will always have a part of us. You will be the keeper of the Murphy family traditions and history. The keeper of the Stones of Burren Bay."

"I will miss you," Oonagh said looking longingly at the small, wrinkled face. Her grandmother had aged quickly over the last few years and Oonagh wondered how she would cope without her.

"And I you, my little treasure. But we will only be separated by miles. That is all." Nan took a big deep breath and stood up. "Now, it is time for you to make me that cup of tea. I fear I'm chilled to the bone." Oonagh grabbed Nan's arm and wrapped it in her own. The two women walked up the trail back to the farmhouse.

# CHAPTER 25

As the storm approached the jagged shore of Burren Bay, Norie's hand moved slowly, with uncertainty and awkwardness. But as her conscious mind released its hold on her motor memory, her hand began to move more fluidly across the paper. The sketch took shape as she instinctively captured the scene before her. The charcoal became her hand, and her hand became the charcoal, moving over the contour of the trees, the lighthouse, the sky, the storm. Unaware of all of this, Norie's heartbeat slowed, and her breath deepened. And as she drew, she felt her fear and grief, her guilt, rise and fall and shift and change. The blank page no longer terrified her. The darkness and heaviness seeped from her mind and heart, through her hand and onto the page with each stroke of the charcoal leaving a feeling of relief. Of love. She could sense the girl standing close by and when she looked up at her, there was love in her eyes too. An artist from another time and place, but nonetheless a kindred soul.

Norie was only vaguely aware of the nearness of thunder and lightning until a gust of wind caught the corner of the pad of paper she was so intently working on. She looked up and saw Wil struggling to run in the wind toward her across the stone pavement. When she reached the rock, Norie made room for her in the scant shelter of the trees. The girl stood close by.

"The storm is really picking up. The power is out in the village," Wil shouted over the din of the wind. "We really should go back to the house." Norie began to stuff her supplies into the backpack preparing to make the run across to the path back to the tearoom. Wil stood, her back to the lighthouse, and yelled toward Norie. "This is going to be a big storm! Maybe we'll finally get some relief from the heat." Norie nodded and glanced toward the girl standing still and watchful beyond Wil. Until now she had been motionless and smiling—peacefully witnessing Norie fall in love with drawing all over again. Now, however, her eyes frantically shifted from Norie to the break in the tree line. Norie stood to look beyond Wil and saw Alice exit the path and head toward the lighthouse. Wil followed Norie's gaze and yelled over the wind.

"What's your mother doing?"

"I don't know."

They stood watching her make her way, her gaunt form fighting the wind, past the lighthouse towards the edge of the cliff. The girl flitted quickly in and around Norie and Wil trying desperately to move them to action. Then Norie understood. She knew exactly where her mother was going. She knew exactly what she was going to do. She remembered seeing her mother take this walk earlier in the summer. Everything her mother had done since their arrival in Burren Bay, her withdrawal, her admissions of guilt, her endless hours of sleep, her poor hygiene, her hair cut, all of it led to this. Suicidal ideation her health teacher had called it. When Alice gave Norie the sketch it was the last step in her preparation. All the signs had been there, but Norie couldn't see through her own pain and self-pity. But now that she could, she had to act. She slipped the backpack on her back. "Go get your mother and Gibson!"

Wil froze, looking in confusion at Norie and across the pavement to Alice.

"Go!" She screamed and Wil leapt into action running full tilt toward the path that Alice had exited seconds before.

Norie and the girl made their way toward Alice who moved at a surprising speed considering her frail state. She called to her mother as she ran, but the wind and thunder swallowed her voice. It seemed like forever before Norie caught up with Alice. Again, the spirit flew quickly between and around them, unable to exert a physical force.

"Mom!" Alice was unaware of Norie's presence. When she noticed her frantically run towards her, she quickened her pace toward the cliff's edge.

"Mom! No! Don't!" Norie pleaded as she covered the last few yards between them looking to the girl for help and then realizing the spirit could do nothing. "Wait! I just want to talk." Close enough now, Norie grabbed her mother's arm. Her mother turned to her angrily.

"The time for talk is over, Norie! I should have done this years ago. Before I had you and ruined everything for you. I should have had the courage then. Just let me go. You'll be better off without me." She pulled away and Norie lost her grip. They were close enough to the edge that Norie feared she would be pulled over with her if she tried to grab her again. She prayed she wouldn't have to make the decision not to.

"I won't be better off without you. Just come away from the edge and we can talk. I promise, we will just talk." Alice stood her ground.

"It hurts too much Norie. I can't go on like this. What kind of life is this for you? I can't be the mother I'm supposed to be. I've failed you. I've failed your father. I've failed your grandmother." She turned back toward the cliff edge, toward the black waves below. "I've failed myself."

Suddenly the spirit flew to the edge and, as if she was harnessing the wind, hovered in the air above the precipice, above the roiling waves, floating above Norie and her mother like a banshee—a woman of the otherworld wailing and keening—warning Alice back away from the brink. Automatically, Alice retreated, positioning herself between Norie and the girl, protecting her from this horrific apparition. The spirit moved slowly toward them, forcing them back to the safety of the lighthouse wall. Alice stood her ground, the fierce instinct to protect her daughter evident in her bold posture. Once she sensed the moment had shifted, that Alice's resolve to hurt herself had faltered, the spirit began to descend to the ground, still and quiet. Norie understood.

Her mother turned around, her back to the cliff edge. They threw their arms around each other and ran toward the door of the lighthouse. At the main entrance the rain began. At first it came down in slow large drops that fell heavy onto the ground around them. Just as they tucked under the eve above the door, the rain began in earnest. Norie and her mother hurried into the small porch and collapsed to the floor in front of the counter Norie had spent hours working at.

"What was that thing?" Alice was still holding tightly to Norie's hand. Norie glanced back toward the door, but the girl was nowhere to be seen. She turned to her mother and spoke.

"I'm not sure you would believe me if I told you." Alice looked away shell-shocked, still frightened by the spirit's show of force. "It doesn't matter anyway. What's important is you tried to protect me, Mom. You were the mother you thought you couldn't be!" Norie was overcome with the same sense of love she had a few minutes before while working the charcoal across the paper.

"You should have just let me go," Alice managed to say, her voice a mere whisper. Alice released Norie and pulled her knees to her chest and wrapped her arms around them. Norie sat feeling the immediate panic subside, but now not knowing what to say or do. She slipped the backpack off her shoulders letting it fall to the ground. The tea tin filled with charcoal and tools clattered against the stone floor. Norie rubbed her hand against her wet, cold body. She felt the pouch around her neck tucked safely under her shirt. Suddenly she had an idea. Pulling it out, she opened the pouch and spilled the stones into the palm of her hand. She closed her fingers around them, held them to her chest and slid along the floor toward her mother.

"I didn't get to thank you for the sketch you gave me." Her mother didn't respond, her face was buried in the crook of her arm. "I didn't remember Grandma Johanna's backyard until that sketch." She paused for a moment. "It was beautiful." Alice raised her head.

"It was from a different time. A happier time."

"We could have that again."

"Norie, I—"

"It's not going to be easy. I know." Norie continued, "We've lost Dad. We've lost Grandma Johanna," she paused, swallowing the emotions that threatened to silence her. "Let's not lose each other."

"Norie, I'm damaged. I'm sick. I've been this way my whole life. I've struggled and struggled, and I'm tired. Your father tried to help me. In the beginning after we had you, but he had his own issues, his own demons. And then you grew up and didn't need me anymore. And when I could have kept your secret, I didn't. I wanted to hurt your father the way he hurt me. I thought I could keep him from taking the art box from you. I thought I could show him that I was your protector and that I had raised you to stand on your own two feet. That just backfired. What can I offer you now?"

"See these stones?" Norie opened the palm of her hand. Alice peered into it while the rain pounded against the porch roof. "These are hard and strong even though they're small. And they're different from each other too." For the first time Norie really noticed how unique the rocks were from one another. One was white and smooth, the second sharp and blackened and the third had tiny fossil fragments embedded in it. "They're probably broken off the rock along this cliff. Maybe from the ice one winter. Or maybe they were dragged here from some place far away when the glaciers moved millions of years ago. But the point is, they're still here. And you and I are still here. We're what's left of this family. And we're both alive."

Alice began to cry. Norie wasn't sure if she was making sense, if she was changing her mother's mind or making things worse, until Alice grabbed her and pulled her onto her lap into her arms. It had been a long time since she felt her mother's arms around her, cradling her like a small child. Her 15-year-old body, though, knew this is where she belonged, where she should have been all along. Norie buried her head in her mother's embrace and began to cry.

By the time Dahlia, Gibson and Wil found them, the storm had passed, and the rain had become a gentle shower. The lichen and small bushes growing on and between the grikes and clints looked plump and fresh against the rock. The trees too, looked as if they had been dusted, their verdant branches reaching up and outwards. Gibson moved to help Alice stand and supported her as they moved out of the lighthouse. Norie returned the stones to the pouch and lifted her backpack onto her shoulders. She looked back over the water as they left the lighthouse. At the edge of the trees near her rock she thought she saw the figure of a girl gazing out over Burren Bay, but as the sunlight broke through the clouds the mirage disappeared. With Gibson on one side of her mom, Norie took her mother's other hand, and they led her back to the tearoom.

Later, as her mother slept more peacefully than she had in months, Norie felt at ease with her hands wrapped around a hot mug of tea. She and her mother still had miles to go on their healing journey, she knew that now. But here in the kitchen of *The Jolly Pot Tearoom and Gift Shop*, amongst the loose-leaf tea and baked goods she felt like she belonged. Belonged around the table with Dahlia, Gibson, and Wil planning the next day's food and drink. Belonged to the lighthouse and the clints and grikes surrounding it. Belonged to her rock, her sacred space. Belonged to the three stones of Burren Bay nestled in a pouch around her neck.

# CHAPTER 26

Norie cleared the trees and adjusted the backpack on her back. She could feel the tea tin nestled at the bottom of the bag—another artist's toolbox with bits and pieces of a creative life once lived on the cliffs of Burren Bay. How long ago, she might never know, but Dahlia helped her to understand that she and the spirit of that artist were connected.

"I don't believe the girl you and your mother saw is simply a ghost wandering the cliffs of the lighthouse because of some unresolved tragedy," Dahlia told them, "I think she appeared to you—crossed through the thin veil between her time and your time—to help you get back the things you lost and the things you were struggling with."

Norie understood that the spirit guided her to reconnect with a part of her she had shunned. Norie needed to embrace her artistic self to begin to heal and move forward. The spirit guide helped her through her own selfish guilt and grief to see her mother's pain and hopelessness. In the end, the guide saved both Norie and Alice, turning mother and daughter toward each other.

"Will she come back? Will she always be there for me," Norie asked. Dahlia wasn't sure. But it didn't matter. She appeared when Norie needed her the most. She had given her the gifts of tone and texture, shape and line, and form and space. She had given her perspective.

She'd have to get a better artist's box though. The tea tin was way too small. Moving forward along the rocky pavement, Norie felt the weight of the new art supplies Gibson had picked up for her in Prosper Bay and she smiled. It felt so good to be drawing again.

It was almost lunchtime and she and Wil agreed to meet at the lighthouse when their chores were done. August had proven to be a month of blissful weather. The storm during the last week of July had cleared the heat and humidity from the air leaving warm, pleasant late summer days. Dahlia said that the September long weekend would be the last weekend they would see any tourists at the tearoom and lighthouse museum. Things tended to shut down on the Island after that as tourists and seasonal residents returned home, to work and school. Norie and her mother would be leaving Burren Bay too, at least for the winter. They would be back though. They belonged here with this new chosen family of theirs.

Norie walked along the tree line to her sacred spot and sat down on the rock warmed by the sun. She managed to grab some alone time to draw at the rock every day. She looked out across the cliff and beyond to the water and took a deep breath. The beauty in front of her had less to do with what she saw and more to do with what she knew she could create from it. She thought of Gram. Gram would have understood that kind of beauty. She thought her mom would too. Alice had been an artist after all and could learn to be an artist again.

It would take time. Norie understood that now. Grief was

complicated and mental health even more so. Her fists still clenched involuntarily when she thought of the accident—when she thought about her father. But with support, empathy and a little self-love Norie knew there was hope for her mother and herself at the end of it all. And art. She always had art. They always had art.

She noticed Wil standing at the door of the lighthouse looking toward the path from the tearoom. I'm probably late, she thought and got up and headed toward the lighthouse. Wil spotted her, waved and then moved quickly back into the porch, closing the door. She is one strange girl sometimes, Norie laughed to herself, but she knew Wil's heart and that made her a great friend. Her first true friend.

As she approached the front door of the lighthouse, she thought she could hear voices inside. The museum and tearoom were closed today. They were always closed on Monday to make up for being open for the other six days of the week. Mondays weren't usually busy in the village either so why a surprise tour group today? She opened the door and stepped into the entrance way. As she made her way through the kitchen to the dining and sitting rooms, she was met with a misfit choir of voices singing "Happy Birthday!"

Sitting around the main room of the lighthouse were her friends and family—her mother, Dahlia and Gibson, Wil, Nell, and even Ray was there. The table was loaded with platters of vegetables and dip, sandwiches and pickles. In the middle sat a large slab cake with Norie's name on it and a beautiful icing photograph of the lighthouse and bay. On the sideboard were gifts wrapped in bright colours and ribbons.

"But it's not my birthday until Friday," Norie exclaimed.

"We couldn't wait until Friday," said Wil and everyone laughed. "Okay, I couldn't wait until Friday. Besides today is our day off and we wanted to really have time to throw a great party!" Everyone clapped and agreed. Norie couldn't remember ever having a surprise birthday party for herself. She teared up as she moved around the room hugging and thanking everyone.

"Should we eat or open the gifts first?" Alice stood beside Norie, her arm loosely draped across her daughter's shoulders. Norie sank into her mother's arm, enjoying the feeling of Alice's skin against hers. She felt like a small child again finding comfort in a hug.

"Open the gifts! Open the gifts!" Wil was more excited than Norie as she took Norie's hand and pulled her to a seat at the head of the table. "Open this one first." Norie smiled as Wil handed her a small gift bag stuffed with tissue. Inside was a small, thin tin palette of handmade mineral watercolour paints. The colours were earthy tones of brown, green and gold.

"I picked it up in Prosper Bay. I hope you like it," said Wil.

"I love it! These colours are so unique." Nell was next to give her a gift and she placed a large blue case that looked like an oversized toolbox on the table in front of Norie.

"This is for you with an explanation," she said, smiling slyly. "But open it first."

Norie stood to flip the latches on the case and lifted the lid. Inside was a selection of paint brushes: a large, wide angled brush like the kind a house painter uses, a thinner brush still larger than a typical artist's paint brush and a collection of assorted artist's brushes of various sizes and shapes. There was a package of painter's rags, a roll of green tape and a large drop cloth. Packages of carpenter's pencils, grease pencils and chalk, and soft pastels also filled the bottom of the box. Norie wasn't sure what to make of this gift. She looked up at Nell with questioning eyes.

"So, as you know I did the mural on the wall of the general store in town." Norie nodded. "Well, I have been approached by the *Friends of the Burren Bay Lighthouse* to do a mural on the wall of this lighthouse keeper's house."

"That's wonderful!" Norie couldn't wait to see what Nell would come up with. Everyone around the room was congratulating Nell for the opportunity.

"Well, it is wonderful, but I won't have time to do it because I am involved in another major project over the winter. I will, however, have time to mentor a protégé for this project." She turned toward Norie. "What do you think about spending the winter designing a mural and painting it next summer here at the museum?" Everyone was super excited now. Norie wasn't sure. She'd never done anything like that before. Nell saw the uncertainty in her eyes and added, "I'll take you through every stage. I really believe you can do this. And—," she paused while the room quieted. "You will be paid rather handsomely for your hard work. You'll be a working artist! What do you say?" Everyone was congratulating Norie and encouraging her to say yes.

Gram would be so proud of her if she took this challenge. In fact, Norie felt that accepting the challenge is what she had to do to honour her grandmother and maybe make up for losing the art box she was entrusted with.

"I'll give it a try!" Norie was excited, but added, "But I'm counting on you to teach me the ins and outs of mural painting."

"It's a deal!" The two shook hands and then Nell gathered Norie into a huge hug.

"There's one more gift," said Wil still full of birthday excitement. "This is from your mom, my mom, Ray and Gib." She handed Norie a gift about the size of a shoebox. It was wrapped in bright paper that looked hand stamped and was tied with a ribbon of beaded twine.

"My sister made the paper and ribbon," said Ray. "She's really crafty."

"It's beautiful." Norie removed the card carefully tucked into the twine. It was handmade using the same light blue cardstock as the sympathy card Dahlia sent months ago. It was that card that brought her and her mother to this moment. This new card had a simple but beautiful drawing of flowers—daffodils, tulips and irises.

"Your mom drew the flowers on the cover," said Dahlia. Norie looked at her mother and smiled.

"It feels good to draw again," her mother said. Norie smiled and nodded. There was definitely more to her mother than she had previously been aware of. It was time the two of them really got to know each other.

Norie opened the card and read it aloud. "For every storm, may you have a rainbow, for every tear, a smile, for every care, a promise and a blessing in each trial. For every problem life sends, a faithful friend to share, for every sign a sweet song, and an answer for each prayer. Happy birthday Norie. Love Mom, Ray, Dahlia and Gibson." Feeling quite emotional, Norie busied herself with untying the twine that held the paper on the gift.

"I don't want to tear the paper. It is so pretty." As the paper fell away, Norie saw a long, narrow, wooden box beneath. It was clearly handmade, the amber wood finely cut and sanded silky smooth. The grain ran lengthwise along the sides of the box to the dovetailed corners with their pins and tails fitted snugly into each other. The lid was held in place by two small brass hinges and held shut with a brass latch.

Norie couldn't speak. Tears rolled down her cheeks and she wiped them away with a napkin.

"We had Ray make the box to replace the one you lost in the fire." Alice's voice shook with emotion. "Besides," she smiled, "the tea tin is too small to hold most of the stuff we saw in Nell's studio." Norie laughed at her mother's attempt to lighten the moment. She ran her fingers across the lid and over the cool brass fittings.

"It's just gorgeous." She could imagine the lopsided grin Gram would have had on her face at the sight of this new, handcrafted artist's toolbox. "It's perfect!" She again moved around the room thanking everyone with hugs and kind words.

"Now it's time to eat," declared Wil. While everyone grabbed a plate and started serving themselves, Norie reached for her backpack and removed the loose pencils and miscellaneous supplies, along with the tea tin that sat on the bottom of the bag. Norie opened the wooden box and added the supplies. She pried the lid off the tea tin and emptied the charcoal, stump, and feathers into the box as well. Then replacing the lid, she sat the tea tin on the sideboard beside the teapot shaped candle tin.

"It looks good there," Wil said.

Then Norie removed the pouch carrying the three stones from around her neck and tucked it into the corner of the box. Now everything was exactly where it belonged.

END

# Acknowledgements

*The Stones of Burren Bay* has come into being like sedimentary rock—bits and pieces of stuff blown together over years into layers of character and plot, setting and theme, and then heated and compressed by the warmth and weight of editing and revision. There are pieces of many people gathered into the strata of this book. From gigantic boulders, to fossils, to microscopic organic particles, each one has been fundamental to the story's creation.

Firstly, I wish to extend my thanks to the Ontario Arts Council for awarding me a Works In Progress Northern Ontario Grant to write this book. While the money was appreciated, the validation of my work really went a long way to keep me writing.

I would like to thank the professionals who have looked at this book at various times during its development: Humber School for Writers mentor Richard Scrimger, developmental editor Gail Anderson Dargatz and U of T Summer Writing Program facilitator Ann Laurel Carter. To Latitude 46, thank you for taking me on. Thank you to Heather Campbell, Mitchel Gauvin, Madison Dillon, and Lindsay Mayhew. To Dr. Mary Ann Corbiere, Assistant Professor at the University of Sudbury, Indigenous Studies, thank you for editing the Ojibwe language in the book and for helping me to understand the role of language on Manitoulin Island in

1892. Thank you to the many beta-readers who read the manuscript and gave me thoughtful and encouraging feedback: Kelly Beaton (you saw it first), Vera Constantineau, Liisa Kovola, David LeBlanc and Kathy Pitzel.

Thank you to my many writer friends and colleagues at the Sudbury Writers' Guild. You have been a constant for me since I joined in 1994—yes in the last century! Thank you for the encouragement, the knowledge and the experience you freely share with me and each other. You are my first and most important writing community.

Thank you to my family: to my sisters Karen Doucette and Cindy Dumas who have been beta-readers, consultants and cheerleaders; to my children and their partners, Robin and Tom and David and Joaquin, who have been art consultants, editors, publicists, IT lifesavers and webmasters.

Finally, thank you to my husband Michael. You have been my rock—solid, foundational, unwavering in your support. Your steadfast love and faith in my abilities has kept me both grounded and able to metamorphose into the writer I am today.